Sexy Shenanigans.

By Anita Kirk

<u>Dedication</u>

Anita's most popular fan would be her father before he sadly got dementia, and he is now devastatingly blowing in the wind. Anita's family has supported her one hundred percent with her writing, and she thanks them for the encouragement and you for taking the time out of your day to pick her book up and read it.
If you do enjoy reading this book, Anita would really appreciate a good review to show other people that you have enjoyed reading.

Acknowledgments

I would like to thank you for taking the time to pick this book out from the millions of books available out there to read, if you do enjoy reading this book your review would mean the world to Anita Kirk for her to enjoy reading and sharing this book with others on social media or in person would be most appreciated.
Thank you.

There are four romantic, raunchy, comically hilarious, in detail different short stories in this book with the fourth story having horror and romance.

Shenanigans on the beach, fact, or fiction chapters.

Chapter One - Reminiscing.

Chapter Two – Has Megan gone forever?

Chapter Three - They forgot to shut the curtains.

Chapter Four - Everybody discussed Megan and Vinny's sex moves.

Chapter Five - Carol and Colin asked for more sex antics.

Chapter Six - Vinny got stuck inside of Megan.

Chapter Seven - Free fanny hat.

<u>Shenanigans</u>

<u>Fact or fiction prologue.</u>

This story and the other stories in this book are for people over eighteen years of age, as it has got a lot of sex scenes described in detail.

A young couple called Megan and Vinny had a long-term high school relationship until they were forced to split up and lose touch with one another, with Megan being forced to move away for her fathers job, with Megan moving back years later and then finally meeting again years later not knowing that they were not far off neighbours living around the corner from one another without knowing.

Megan invites Vinny into her home for a lot more than a beer, they end up with an audience watching them enjoying themselves in different places with people starting to mirror everything that they do, they then go down to the beach and find out that it is not a normal beach with it being a nudist beach, and the sea is different full of naked sex thirsty bodies on inflatables with them ending up with plenty of new friends with lots of very friendly close touching each other up parties.

They end up on most programmes on the television with beaches named after them, and they love teaching other people, showing them as a couple how to enjoy sex with each other.

They set up a sex shop, and a holiday travel agents called (Shenanigans on the Beach Holidays) providing the full package with the sex hotel/sex plane journey/sex boat rides/sex performances and more with funny things happening through the stories to keep you entertained while you are reading.

(This is story one of four inside of this book.)

The pub chapters.

Chapter One - Tina and Jane pretended to be together.

Chapter Two - What does bondage feel like?

Chapter Three - Tina and Adam's bedroom.

Chapter Four - They had a moving-in party with shenanigans.

The pub prologue.

Tina and Jane find it hard to meet a man with them pretending to be together as a couple giving up on men going to different pubs to hopefully find Mr Right.

Do they finally meet their future lovers to make their lives romantically happy in the bedroom?

They enjoy many parties with bondage and plenty of things going on with them owning horses, enjoying their lives, and starting a new family, maybe, you will have to read to find out.

(This is story two out of four stories inside of this book.)

Foam parties' chapters.

Chapter One - Greg and James's faces lit up as Emma and Lucy walked in.

Chapter Two - Emma and Lucy teased them.

Foam parties' prologue.

Greg and James went to the gym often with them, liking a certain lady each, and wished that they could go out with them for a long time and touch them all over from head to toe.

Lucy and Emma walked into their workplace unexpectedly.

Do Greg and James click with Lucy and Emma?

Do they end up with erotic, sexy play between them?

Do they start a new unique joint sexy business?

(This is story three out of four in this book.)

Fun or not chapters.

Chapter One - Is it a free day trip for a reason?

Chapter Two - They enjoyed each other thinking that it was their last moments alive.

Chapter Three - Do the last four survive?

Chapter Four - Do they get their own back?

Fun or not prologue.

Holidaymakers Shirley and Frank go on a day trip thinking that it would be an enjoyable day out painting houses for a charity, they have an unexpected horror happening to them as they arrive with them all feeling frightened for their lives with plenty of sexy shenanigans happening, also they have got to solve a mystery and a major problem, they soon find out that they are in a life or death situation.

Do any of them survive?

You will have to read to find out.

(This is story four out of four for this book.)

Shenanigans
on the beach/fact or fiction.

Chapter One

Reminiscing.

This is where the erotic story begins five years earlier.

My name is Vinny; I am just over six feet tall and slim with the perfect toned body.

Today is the fifth-year anniversary of the day when I met Megan behind the bike sheds at school to give her our necklace, she ripped the heart-shaped wrapping paper fast to find out what was inside and she happily put the matching necklace around both of our necks, that day we promised not to remove them until the day that we die!"

Megan is five foot six tall; she always looks extra-hot, slim, cute, gorgeous, tall, and sexy, and she is a long-faced softly spoken smiley girl that always loved to wear pink with a small dimple in her chin, she loved life and laughed with people, not at them.

In the winter we built snowmen and in the summer we sunbathed and we could talk to each other about anything and everything, we thought that we would be together forever with us being best friends with benefits, and we hoped to one day be in the Ginny book of world records for something that nobody else has done that was unique.

Even though we had hardly anything, we enjoyed walking around town looking in all of the shops, pretending and boasting about how rich we were

while looking inside of all of
the shops that we passed.

We talked and
dreamed about the business
that we would one day have
with our best friends,
Ghianu and Casey.

Ghianu was six foot
and thin with long legs and
his girlfriend, Casey was
five foot and very slim with
beautiful blue eyes that look
as blue as the sun shining on
the sea, her small nose and
black hair suit her smooth
skinned face.

My parents June and
Tom have got dark brown
hair with a slim build, they

think that it is cute how I had spent every penny on Megan, they always used to reminisce about how they had met in the stand at a crowded football match trying to chat each other up over all of the noise.

On our anniversary, Megan walked up to me crying, announcing that she had to move to Australia with her father John's job, explaining that he was an engineer and they had to leave that evening.

I asked if I could go to her home and wave her off, and she replied yes, Megan's parents, John, and

**Margarita could not
apologise to me enough for
them leaving the country
and separating us.**

Chapter Two

Has Megan gone forever?

We sadly said goodbye
to each other with us both
saying that we would text
each other regularly to keep
in touch with one another.

We stayed connected
for a while, sending each
other sexy loving texts and
hot erotic photos.

Megan suddenly
stopped texting me back,
after a few months, I do not
know why!

Then our friends,
Ghianu and Casey then

announced that they had to move away also with the circus that they had both joined to the other side of Mitty Island, Toke.

I then lost touch with Ghianu and Casey, also nearly completely with just an odd text backwards and forwards to each other.

Five years on.

I think of Megan daily with me being twenty years old, I live in a flat at the other end of Mitty Island, Toke City with me working full-time for myself as an electrician, I am hoping to meet up with Ghianu and Casey now and again.

The weather is always hot here with the sun shining every day where I live with shops and many more places to go, mainly the beaches and a few more years have passed on slowly with me still missing Megan.

I was helping a large company out mending some light switches, and while I was there, a small team of people were mending some doors using a wood plane in the room where I was working.

The aroma of the fresh wood being planed off the door brought back memories of me and Megan doing woodwork lessons back at school with our teacher Mr Jones making all different things with some useful and some not, we made a heart-shaped key ring that I still have got on my keys, Megan's has got a similar design because we made them together with our names burnt into the middle of a heart.

I look at my key ring and reminisce about happy times that have gone by, and I always wonder where she is and what she is doing.

I am just going for a walk to my local supermarket for a few meals.

I have given myself a two-weeks holiday break away from work, my flat is within walking distance of the beach that I have never visited, but I want to hopefully visit with Megan if we ever meet again because I can't stop dreaming about her loving hugs and more with me waking up sweating with my hard as a rock wand tugging myself off regularly squirting my cum into the shower, I always wonder if

she still has got her heart-
wood key ring?

I am walking back
from the supermarket, and
a girl who looks the spitting
image of my Megan is
staring at me from her
downstairs house window
looking puzzled in the face
at me, it is like she is
working out if it is really
me, she is squirting perfume
on herself to make her feel
and smell nice.

I am walking very
slowly past her house
looking back at her, I am
hopeful that it is my Megan.

Her eyes were lit up
brightly, like a light bulb.

She ran to her front
door, opening it, looking at
him, as he was about to
walk past, she realised that
he was her lost love Vinny.

Megan shouted. "Wow,
it is really you Vinny, it is
me Megan, come inside."

Vinny sounded
grateful. "I am glad that
you have still got your
heart-shaped key ring that
we had made at school, look
at mine, it looks as good as
the day that we made them,
yours is pristine as well!"

They discussed how this was
a one-in-a-million chance for
them to meet up again.

Megan sounded giddy. "I
have got a job as a receptionist
at a large factory selling sex toys
called Shenanigans!"

Vinny sounded impressed.
"That sounds like a cool job!"

Megan explained. "It
is, my phone was stolen, so I
devastatingly lost your
number, that is why I lost
touch with you!"

Vinny sounded over the
moon. "I am just happy to
be back with you, I love
your paintings on the wall

of Whitby, North Yorkshire in the United Kingdom and the streets of Spain, they look so beautiful!"

Megan sounded happy." I am glad that you like my paintings, we will hopefully go there on holiday together!"

Vinny asked Megan. "Please swap telephone numbers with me!"

They swapped numbers with each other.

Megan sounded grateful. "I am going to treasure this number on my phone."

Vinny agreed. "Same here, you are the love of my life now and forever, I am sure that we will enjoy many special moments and holidays together in the near future!"

Megan grabbed her necklace on her neck. "Look, I have never removed my necklace from my neck since the day that you had put it on!"

Vinny smiled. "Look, I still have got my necklace, and I have never removed it either!"

They hugged each other and kissed together, carrying on chatting, with Vinny commenting how nice Megan's fruity, fresh smelling perfume was commenting that the smell was a little bit overpowering.

Megan spoke. "I live alone with my parents, John and Margarita; they are temporarily living with me in my two-bedroom detached house until their house is ready to move into when their sale has gone through."

Vinny boasted, "I am looking forward to a few

weeks off work so that we can enjoy some time together, I hope that you don't mind, I will just put my shopping into your fridge, then I will sit on your sofa with you!"

Megan screeched. "I have got two weeks off work as well."

Vinny laughed. "It is strange with us both having time off work at the same time, isn't it?"

Megan walked off, talking. "Yes, but I am glad, I will get a beer for both of us from out of the fridge, we can then feel more chilled!"

Vinny was sitting next to Megan. "Thank you for the beer, and what did the bottle say to the postcard?"

Megan smiled. "I am loving sitting next to you, what is the answer?"

Vinny guessed. "I wish you were beer."

Megan laughed. "Very funny, I am so glad none of us met or wanted anybody else, and I am glad that I have moved back to Mitty Island only a few months ago, when we were apart all I could think about was you while I was away!"

Vinny commented. "If you hadn't been forced to move away, we would have most likely been living together by now!"

Megan held Vinny's hand. "Yes, we can both finally do what we have been longing to do for years, instead of dreaming to sleep together it has become reality, and we can now play with each others' bodies in a comfy bed every day as many times as we like."

Chapter Three

They forgot to shut the curtains.

Vinny kissed Megan. "We will definitely make up for lost time, it made me feel so tired when I worked part-time as a paperboy and did my weights after school in my bedroom when I was a child, but I always made time for you!"

Megan looked up and down at Vinny. "At least you are still as fit and irresistible now as you were when you were fifteen, I am glad that I have moved back to Toke!"

Vinny stroked Megan's arm. "I still feel head over heels in love with you, I loved holding your hands and kissing you."

Megan burst out laughing. "Do you remember the day that you had walked around with spunk on your trousers, you made people guess if it was really spunk and the look of disgrace on some of their faces was so funny?"

Vinny giggled. "It was so good when we used to watch out for each other making a random noise like a fake sneeze or whatever noise we agreed on as a warning of a teacher walking near to the bike sheds, they were the good old days, I am planning a charity event for people who can't ejaculate!"

Megan looked at Vinny with a puzzled look. "What are you talking about?"

Vinny laughed speaking. "Just let me know if you can't cum, I mean ejaculate your juices all over me."

Megan chuckled. "You are funny and daft."

Vinny spoke in a high-pitched voice. "Do you remember when Mr Long nearly caught you sucking my cock behind the bike sheds because Ghianu and Casey were poorly and couldn't do a fake sneeze to warn us that he was there?"

Megan chuckled. "Yes, how could I forget, and I didn't put my breasts away in time, so he couldn't stop full-on looking at my tits!"

They suddenly started to kiss on the large three-seater cream sofa with no ornaments around the room, and a tidy house with clean cream walls and a plain light brown carpet with a small stainless steel silver coffee table next to the sofa.

Vinny kissed Megan's hand. "You are turning me on so much!"

Megan sounded excited. "I feel so excited, I am enjoying touching your trousers where your joystick is!"

Vinny carried Megan upstairs with them kissing on the way up the cream-carpeted steps into her bedroom forgetting to shut the cream curtains, with Vinny putting the radio on a low volume with lots of fast, upbeat music playing, with them carrying on kissing with Vinny removing Megan's black Lacey underwear with his teeth, her skimpy red top, and black shorts with them dancing along to the music in between.

Megan announced. "I am removing your trousers and top."

Vinny sounded in need of some loving. "I think that we are both desperate for each other with how fast we removed each others' clothes!"

They laid on the bed while Vinny licked and

massaged Megan from head to foot, concentrating between her legs the most.

Megan noticed and pointed out, "Look, my neighbours Carol and Collin in the house opposite mine are watching us!"

Vinny commented. "I have no care; I think that it adds to the excitement! "

Megan sounded excited. "I am well turned on; I have been waiting for this moment for years!"

Vinny sounded grateful. "I have been looking forward to this for years as well, I am enjoying licking your hair-free and smooth, sweet-smelling clit and playing with your massive pair of melons with great joy!"

Megan announced smirking. "I have orgasmed so much I am wet through, and I have spurted my cum everywhere, it has covered the bed, so I don't need that invitation in your joke that you cracked earlier!"

Vinny sounded amazed giggling. "I am glad, and I know it is amazing!"

Megan sounded like a kid in a sweet shop. "I am

loving feeling your rock-hard manhood and massaging your mushroom tip with my tongue, I am making it leak a little!"

Vinny looked hot. "It feels like I am going to explode at any second, I will massage between your legs with my cock near to your dew flaps for a while!"

Megan begged. "Please put your hot rod in gently to start with, as it is my first time having sex!"

Vinny sounded incredibly happy. "I agree with it being my first time as well, it is going into your virgin love hole now!"

Megan screamed with pleasure, begging for more.

Vinny closed his eyes with pleasure. "I am moving my penis in and out that fast, it is making me want to ejaculate, so I am removing it to tease you for a while!"

Megan screamed. "Please put it back in soon because you are teasing me now!"

Vinny complimented. "You feel lovely and wet and cosily warm!"

Megan begged. "I think that you have done enough teasing now, please put your penis back inside of my clit!"

Vinny gave in teasing. "Okay, I am going back in now, you are so warm, wet, and tight and it feels lovely in your wet hole."

Megan sounded desperate. "I am grabbing your bottom to try to keep your warm stick up inside of me, my clit is that wet, it is making a wet and sloppy noise!"

Vinny suggested. "At least it is a change from our heavy breathing."

They rolled over a few times, swapping turns on top of each other, with Megan on top for a while with her warm breasts gently bouncing up and down on his chest.

Vinny announced. "I am going to pick your bra up and tie you to the bed with it and blindfold you with your trousers licking your clit, and then I will put my tool into your mouth, after a while you can then get onto all fours with me whipping you with my top!"

Megan panted. "I think that we are both hot and out of breath!"

Vinny smiled. "You love begging for my dick in you, don't you?"

Megan agreed. "Yes, I am begging you to put your cock in now."

Vinny whispered softly in her ear. "I will ram my cock inside of you in a minute when I have finished teasing you!"

Megan sounded incredibly happy. "I love it

when you push your warm
snake in so hard!"

Vinny asked. "Is this
hard enough for you?"

Megan screeched.
"Yes, please put your
yoghurt hose in faster and
faster."

Vinny was amazingly
fast. "This is fun, I am
putting my dick in and out
in rhythm to a fast beat of
the music!"

Megan stared out of
the window. "Look out of
the window, my neighbours
are looking at us still with
their tongues hanging out

and their eyes are popping out of their sockets in shock!"

Vinny did not care. "Let them watch, it looks like they are enjoying it with their eyes and noses glued to the glass."

They were both hot and sweaty with them at their climax.

Vinny announced. "I cannot hold my sperm back any longer, I am ejaculating up into your flaming lips now!"

They saw Carol and Colin clapping through the

window opposite them, giving them a thumbs up, with them stripping off trying to copy what Megan and Vinny had just done, with Carol and Colin looking so hot wiping sweat from their foreheads.

Megan laughed aloud. "Sorry, but I can't stop thinking about how funny Mr Longs' face was as he sent us back to our classes, with his cheeks a little rosy, and his trousers looked a little bit too tight from looking at my massive boobs!"

Vinny agreed. "Yes, it was funny with him being

so embarrassed, with him turning red as a beetroot!"

Megan reminisced. "We had some great times together, in every class that we had together, we always sat at the side of each other, it was hard to separate us!"

Vinny smiled. "At least I never got caught touching you under the table!"

Megan and Vinny were watching Carol and Colin having sex, they discussed that it was like watching a live porn video with Vinny starting to get excited again kissing Megan.

Megan and Vinny were both smiling at Carol and Colin through the window, with them leaning on the glass, they were trying to communicate with each other, holding pretend tits up and moving their hands up and down doing tugging-off sign's movements with their hands between them.

The neighbours could not stop looking at Megan's tits.

They both said how tired they felt, with Megan running a bath for them both to enjoy together washing each others' bodies while still kissing.

After they had got out of the bath and got dressed, Vinny turned the radio off, with Megan asking Vinny if he wanted her to walk him home.

Vinny agreed. "I will just get my shopping from your fridge!"

They left Megan's house.

Megan explained. "It just feels like we were never separated."

Vinny agreed. "I feel like that as well, back at school, it was so much fun, like a cat-and-mouse game with us being the prey behind the bike sheds!"

Megan sounded positive. "At least on the upside, we only got caught once!"

Carol and Colin were looking out of the lounge window, as soon as Vinny and Megan stepped outside, Carol and Colin ran up to them, asking them for a repeat performance soon.

Megan and Vinny said maybe they would soon, waving goodbye.

As they got to Vinny's home, they walked into the kitchen putting the shopping into the fridge with them starting to feel raunchy again wanting more sex, removing their clothes in the doorway walking straight into the bedroom getting onto the bed making the same mistake, not shutting the light brown long curtains, with it looking onto the main outside entrance door to the flats where it was in full view of anybody, and everybody entering the door and more.

Vinny stood up announcing. "I am just

getting the whipped cream out of the fridge and a blue tie from my draw, I will cover your penis fly trap doughnut hole and breasts in the cream, and then I will tie your hands to the bed with my tie out of my draw, then I will lick all of the cream off you with great pleasure!"

Megan smiled. "Your warm long rig is lovely and hard again, I am enjoying every second!"

Megan put the cream onto Vinny's long thick tube, licking every bit off, then sucked it hard with Vinny, slipping his pogo

stick inside of Megan's love
hole while gently stroking
her hair.

Vinny noticed and
pointed out an old couple
looking through the window
at Megan's jugs with their
eyes nearly popping out,
trying to cover the window
with their bodies attracting
attention to other people
when they were trying to do
the opposite.

Chapter Four

Everybody discussed Megan and Vinny's sex moves

Megan looked around the room. "I have just noticed your simple manual abs machine on the floor; can I have a go on it pretty please?"

Vinny nodded yes. "Yes, you may have a go, anything of mine is yours!"

Megan explained. "I am sitting on the flat base of the manual machine pushing myself down with my back, I laid straight back with the back of my head on the floor, I would like it even more if I could suck your dick as I sit up!"

Vinny explained. "I am standing in front of you with my dick smooth and solid, ready for you so that you can still suck my dick off as you sit up!"

Megan sounded happy. "That sounds really cool."

Vinny commented. "We should make this a regular activity as it is fun, and you get a little extra exercise at the same time to keep your gorgeous body fit, and I get plenty of enjoyment as well!"

More people appeared, looking through the window looking goggle eyed.

Megan and Vinny just laughed together, saying that it was different with it feeling like they were on the inside of a goldfish bowl.

Megan suggested. "We have done it before at my home, so let's just carry on, it is exciting and adventurous being watched!"

People were tapping on the window at them shouting go for it, lovely jugs, and other random comments drooling with their eyes nearly popping out, attracting more people.

Vinny sucked her nipples, feeling how smooth and erect her baps were, he then entered her rear with his knob, ejaculating his cum into Megan's rear end.

Megan sounded incredibly happy. "That felt amazing!"

Vinny beamed. "Your tits are such a turn-on alone, with more than a handful, and your nipples feel lovely and hard!"

The crowd were
shouting how much they
had enjoyed their erotic sex,
clapping and asking for
some more sexy
entertainment soon with big
smiles on their faces.

Megan suggested.
"Let's have another bath
here and wash each other
gently!"

Vinny sounded happy.
"I think that we have both
enjoyed that bath, we can
now watch a sexy film while
drinking wine!"

Megan suggested.
"Let's go for a walk to the

local pub now that the film has finished."

Vinny dreamed. "I am sure that we will be married and have children together one day!"

Megan agreed. "I hope so, I am enjoying our walk to the pub!"

Vinny walked faster. "Me too, at least we are here now!"

Everybody in the pub were drinking at the bar, people serving were all discussing Megan and Vinny and their erotic sex moves.

Megan and Vinny sat down with everybody wanting to buy them a drink, with them staying for a few hours with plenty of free drinks provided by generous customers, this made them feel a little bit tipsy.

Vinny suggested. "Let's strip off and see how many people do the same!"

Megan agreed. "Why not?"

There was a growing crowd after hearing their conversation with them stripping off in front of the whole pub.

Vinny mentioned. "This is going to be interesting!"

Megan announced. "I am going to enjoy sucking your dick, it is better than sucking a lollipop!"

Vinny looked up and down at Megan's body. "I enjoy everything about your beautiful body!"

Megan knelt down and sucked Vinny's dick with everybody, egging them on.

Vinny laid on a table in the bar with Megan getting on top of him and moving his dick in and out of her pussy lips, he then fingered her while massaging the whole of her body with his prick.

They then moved onto a large cream, soft cushioned bench that was a little bit comfier.

Everybody could not believe what they were seeing getting turned on asking each other if they wanted to join in with them.

A customer said. "I really hope that the police

do not walk inside of this pub at this moment in time, or it would be embarrassing with most of us probably getting arrested with people stripping off and copying what you are both doing!"

People were just tossing themselves off with many people on top of the tables, with the tables making plenty of creaking noises.

There was a sudden crash with a couple that was on top of a table that were still enjoying sex, with the table legs giving way onto the floor.

Most people carried on with what they were doing, just looking and shouting. "Are you okay?"

Some people laughed.

Megan smiled. "I hope that they are okay, at least we have got table legs to play with as well now, my dad and I are building a table, and we are currently shaping the legs, he said the last time that I got a pair of legs I married them!"

Vinny laughed, then put his cock back inside of Megan and slowly pushed in and out of her moist warm hole, getting faster and spurting up inside of her warm vagina.

Everybody clapped as he had cum.

Vinny and Megan then thanked everyone for the drinks, they waved goodbye and then went back to Vinny's home for another bath together, they then got into bed talking about how exciting it was, keeping close to one another with them drifting off to sleep cuddling one another.

The next morning as they woke, Vinny got out of bed and opened the curtains letting the sunshine in, with him just wearing a pair of boxer shorts getting back into bed to wake her gently, with him starting to touch her under the covers, as she was about to go into the bathroom to get dressed she decided not to bother getting out of bed, and removed his boxer shorts under the covers massaging the end of his soft log with her tongue, then sucked his stick hard, with Vinny putting a few fingers into her warm wet hole fingering her in return.

Vinny sucked Megan's snuggle pups, then gave her a love bite on her neck with them noticing that they had an audience again, with him pushing his hot rod into Megan's anus moving in and out fast, with Megan feeling elated while still fingering her at the same time with his special magic long warm fingers that felt amazing.

Megan tapped Vinny, shouting. "Please push harder!"

Vinny removed his moist hard warm weapon moving onto Megan's snake charmer sucking her, honker honker's at the same time with him announcing that he was about to spurt asking

Megan to finish it off with her hands, with her holding his dick with her hand moving up and down on his knob pointing it at her over-sized buoyancy aids.

Megan asked. "Can I please measure how long your love machine is when it is not solid and also when it is?"

Vinny nodded yes. "Course you can, my love!"

Megan picked up his tape measure that was at the side of the bed, measuring it at six inches long.

Vinny quizzed. "How long is it not erected?"

Megan proudly announced. "It is an ideal size for my cum hole six inches, but I think you have not gone soft properly yet, I think that you need to cum again!"

Vinny and Megan were hot and sweaty but started touching each other again.

Megan sounded breathless. "I am not complaining because we have got a lot to catch up on!"

Megan used her hands with his penis growing larger with her getting the tape measure again.

Vinny spoke. "So, you are measuring it again."

Megan laughed. "Yes, you are nearly seven inches now, you are like a battery, you just keep going with sperm available on demand!"

Vinny moved back into her cupids cupboard for a while screwing her good and proper, pulling his warm screwdriver out again with her using her hands again, with him fingering her while she jerked him off carrying on using her hand pointing his cock towards her pair of buns with a skin cherry on top of each of them, with him getting near to his crowning point with sperm covering her top half like a necklace.

The crowd outside were speaking very loudly, asking if they could join in next time, with Megan and Vinny reading their lips.

They discussed that they were not sure if they were serious, or joking, with their reply being a no thank you, they then had a warm bath and food then shut the curtains and talked for a while with gentle candlelight around them, they then went back to the pub finding out that they were still the talk of the town.

Chapter Five

Carol and Colin asked for more sex antics in the pub.

Megan mentioned. "Do you know if Ghianu and Casey are still together?"

Vinny mentioned. "They were moving around with the circus the last time that I knew anything!"

A man mentioned to Megan. "I overheard your conversation; I have not seen your friends Ghianu and Casey for a while in here to have a drink and chat with them!"

Vinny suggested. "I hope that they are okay, let's go back to your home, Megan, for a rest!"

They walked to Megan's home.

Megan's father, John, spoke. "Me and your mother have just been talking about you!"

Vinny mentioned. "I thought our ears were burning, I hope that it was nothing bad!"

Megan's mum replied. "We were talking about how happy you looked lately and about the area being nice and there are plenty of friendly people around here!"

Megan sounded attached. "I personally think that it is better living here!"

John sounded unsure. "I am not sure if I like it better in Australia yet, but I am sure I will be happy living here!"

Megan's mum, Margarita, voiced her opinion. "I do miss Australia, but I like being here too!"

John had excitement in his voice. "I cannot wait to move into our new home down the road when it is ready for us to move into."

There was a knock at the door.

Megan's mum Margarita answered leaving the door open looking puzzled speaking to Megan. "Carol and Colin from next door are at the door asking for more erotic sex antics from you both!"

Vinny and Megan looked at her a little flushed in the face with a blank look.

Megan mentioned. "Just tell them that we will speak to them later!"

John questioned Megan. "What were they talking about?"

Megan did not say anything with her not knowing what to say changing the subject. "At least me and Vinny are back together!"

Margarita announced. "We are both glad that you are back together because you never stopped talking about him and you would never remove your necklace, and you always panicked if you could not find your wood key ring, and you regularly got upset complaining because you had lost his phone number a few months after you had left!"

Vinny sounded grateful. "I am super happy that you flew back, Megan, or we may have lived a miserable life alone!"

Megan agreed, with a tear of happiness rolling down her face.

John sounded surprised. "I am still

amazed how you have met up again."

Vinny suggested to Megan. "Do you want to go upstairs for a lie down because I think we could both do with a rest on your bed?"

Megan agreed. "Yes, that sounds good."

Vinny suggested. "We can both enjoy some television while we go upstairs if you like!"

Megan asked. "Carry me upstairs please, then put me on to the bed!"

Vinny announced. "Now that I have shut the door, I will kiss you while we strip each others clothes off!"

Megan asked. "Please finger me now that we are both in our birthday suits!"

Vinny mentioned. "That conversation was a little bit difficult downstairs, but at least we are enjoying each other now, I am loving putting my fingers inside of your pussy!"

Megan mentioned. "At least we have got a little bit

of time away from my parents for the moment."

Vinny whispered. "I hope that they cannot hear us!"

Megan did not sound bothered. "My parents will be moving into their own home soon, this vibrator that I have just got out of my bedside cabinet draw has never been used, I got it free when I started my receptionist job at Shenanigans."

Vinny sounded surprised. "What a great freebie to try."

Megan demanded. "Put your warm middle leg inside of my vagina, and the vibrator in my ass at the same time whilst I am laying on the bed with my anus on the bed with my legs wide open ready for you!"

Vinny agreed. "Oh yes, I will do that, no problem!"

Megan suggested. "That feels so good, I will massage your body at the same time!"

Vinny mentioned. "I will massage you from head to foot with my dick and finally arrive in your sugar hole!"

They finally stood up, leaning against the bed with him thrusting his fat stick inside of her deep bullet hole while putting the vibrator up her bum again pushing them both inside of her at the same time.

Carol and Colin were looking into the window again, looking wet through having sex, also in front of Megan and Vinny.

Megan smiled at Carol and Colin at what they were doing, with them getting carried away with one another, giving them a thumbs up.

Vinny ejaculated his love juice inside of Megan, trying to pull his magic wand out of Megan's doughnut hole with them locked together with his pocket rocket locked tight stuck up inside of her.

They panicked, trying to get the attention of the neighbours through the window waving erratically for help, hoping that they noticed them and called for an ambulance.

They carried on waving, standing with a thumbs up back from Carol and Colin with them totally oblivious of the situation.

Carol and Colin had finally noticed that Megan and Vinny had been in the same position for a long time, leaning on the bed without moving as they had finally finished having sex, knocking on Megan's front door again.

Megan shouted downstairs to please let them in if it was Carol and Colin from next door and let them upstairs into her room.

Megan's father, John, shouted. "OK." Back to Megan, then answered the door, letting them in with them walking upstairs into Megan's room, as soon as they walked inside, they could not stop laughing with them standing up stuck together in front of them at the side of the bed.

Megan sounded panicked explaining. "Could you please phone an ambulance because we are both stuck together good and proper, and we are not able to separate apart because Vinny's cock is stuck inside of my cum hole still?"

Margarita and John knocked on Megan's bedroom door, and they were about to walk into her room wanting to know what was going on.

Carol opened the door a jar poking her head around the door and stopped them from entering by saying that they were telling each other jokes while trying not to laugh, saying that they were just chilling out and messing around and for them to go out, or make themselves a cup of tea.

Margarita and John went back downstairs loudly, discussing that they thought that they were not telling the truth.

Carol phoned for the ambulance with it arriving promptly, the ambulance ladies walked upstairs putting a blanket around their naked bodies with them still stuck together trying not to laugh, with them struggling to take them downstairs and transport them into the ambulance on a large stretcher.

Margarita and John stood looking in shock at them, they were lost for words with a comment saying that she knew that they were not telling the truth.

The ambulance set off taking them to the hospital on the stretcher with them stuck together, with them nearly falling off, with them still trying not to laugh with her colleague cracking jokes most of the way to the hospital.

One ambulance lady said. "What do a penis and a Rubik's cube have in common?"

Vinny replied in a fed-up tone of voice. "I have got no idea!"

She answered: "The more you play with it, the harder it gets."

Laughter with Megan and Vinny joining in.

The other ambulance lady cracked a joke saying. "What did one saggy boob say to the other?"

They all did not know.

She said the answer. "If we don't get some support, people will think that we are nuts."

Megan laughed. "Very funny."

Chapter Six

Vinny got stuck inside of Megan

They heard the
ambulance driver let staff
from the hospital know that
they were on their way,
explaining what had
happened.

Laughter was very loud
from the hospitals side of
the radio, with the person
from the other side of the
radio cracking a joke.
"What do you call a
guy with a small dick?"

They did not know the
answer.

He announced the answer. "Just in."

"Laughter."

As they had nearly arrived, Megan cracked a joke. "Why does Father Christmas have such a big sack?"

Nobody knew the answer.

She answered. "Because he only comes once a year."

They all had enjoyed their little jokes, the staff at the hospital were waiting for them standing outside of the ambulance trying not to laugh at them.

As they arrived in the cubicle, staff, patients, and visitors were constantly opening the curtain for a nosy, with other random people looking around the curtain at them laughing and talking with them announcing how gobsmacked they were at what they were seeing.

The staff put washing up liquid on the sex stick area the best that they could with no good result, telling them to stick it out for a few hours, laughing still at their own joke that they had just announced fitting it into the conversation.

Megan and Vinny looked at one another talking to each other about what a mess that they had got themselves into, with them laid down talking about how uncomfortable they felt with a few blankets on, and they were around every part that the staff could cover, with the blankets around them falling off them now and again, with them trying to keep them over them for their dignity and privacy, and they kept them warm.

One hour later.

Megan's polo hole let
Vinny's dick free finally
with them, telling the staff
with a loud. "Hurray."
Coming from many people.

The hospital staff gave
them a clean blanket each
trying not to laugh sending
them home in a taxi back to
Vinny's home with them
feeling a little shocked at
what had just happened
with them having a bath
together, they then had a lie
down falling asleep holding
each other for a while.

As they woke, Megan mentioned. "I think that it would be nice to go to the beach for a change of scenery!"

After a discussion between them, they decided to go down to the beach to sunbathe with them packing a towel and sunscreen in a bag each from their separate homes.

Vinny sounded interested. "I am looking forward to sunbathing and a relaxing afternoon chilling out, don't forget to lock your door, Megan, before we go."

Carol and Colin left their home front door, knocking on Megan's door.

Carol asked. "How did you both get on at the hospital?"

Megan and Vinny were starting to explain that if they ever got into the same situation not to bother going to the hospital because they did nothing apart from using a little bit of washing up liquid, and they had just laughed at them cracking rubbish jokes with half of the hospital looking in at them.

Colin laughed. "No, we will just get you help if it ever happens to us."

Carol mentioned. "What did the fish say when it swam into the wall?"

Vinny quizzed. "What is the answer?"

Carol answered. "Dam."

Megan laughed. "Very funny Carol!"

Carol sounded happy. "I am glad that you enjoyed my joke, me and Colin are going to book a very long holiday away!"

Vinny smiled. "You do right to enjoy yourselves, life is too short not to enjoy yourselves!"

Carol and Colin waved goodbye.

Megan and Vinny waved back to them, saying. "See you later and enjoy your holiday." They then left.

Vinny dribbled over Megan's naked body while she put on her bikini, with them walking back downstairs, Megan locked the front door, and then

they walked down to the
beach.

Vinny and Megan
arrived at the beach,
realising that it was called
Bloom Nudist Beach, with
them sharing that they both
felt a little bit nervous
having to strip their clothes
off in front of larger crowds
of people.

A male holidaymaker
who was going home had
stopped to talk with them.
"Me and my friends will be
coming with me next time, I
hope that you enjoy the

beach as much as I did with lots of unpredictability and plenty of sexy things going on, my advice is that you go onto the floats in the sea!"

Megan mentioned. "I am sure that we will enjoy ourselves, I have got a joke, what do you call a can opener that doesn't work?"

The man asked. "What is the answer?

Megan answered. "A can't opener."

Vinny laughed. "You are funny."

The man giggled. "Yes, that was funny, I have got to go now, enjoy yourselves, bye!"

Megan replied to the man. "Bye."

As they arrived on the hot sandy Bloom beach, they were looking around noticing that there were naked bodies everywhere and people on the floats in the sea were getting distracted by the notice board on the bar advertising alcoholic Qui and blue rock cool, with them both on offer on a two for one deal.

Megan walked over to the bar. "Please, can I purchase two drinks of Qui!"

Vinny put their towels on the hot dry sand after a few hours of drinking and sunbathing, they had forgotten what had happened earlier with a few drinks inside of them, with them being chilled out starting to kiss with passion and caress one another gently tickling and touching each other all over.

Vinny announced. "I think that we are the only people that have got bits of clothing on, so I am going to put my hands down your bikini top and touch your cream buns at the same time!"

Megan mentioned. "The grains of sand make everything feel grainy with the sand being on everything!"

Vinny suggested. "Yes, it can be a little bit annoying with everything feeling gritty."

Megan put her hands down Vinny's shorts, touching his just over six inches hard as a rock prick.

Vinny looked into the sea. "Look on that extra-large float in the sea, there is a lady sucking a mans dick!"

Megan announced. "They look like our old school friends Ghianu and Casey!"

Chapter Seven

Free fanny hat

Megan agreed with them both, laughing and looking a little puzzled together, staring at them in the sea from a distance.

Vinny removed Megan's bikini top, kissing, sucking, and playing with her coconuts, loving every second.

Megan looked warm in the face. "I feel turned on so much, and I can feel eyes on us from an old couple sitting at the side of us!"

Vinny pointed out. "They look like they are happy watching the world go by kissing one another gently on the lips with their private parts hanging freely, they are obviously getting a buzz from watching us with them smiling a lot!"

Megan looked at the couple. "They have got a large beach bag at the side of them on their towel with them sat chatting on the beach from a distance, their eyes are completely glued to us."

Vinny turned his head towards them and looked at

them smiling, saying. "This will make them stare even more!"

Vinny put his hands down Megan's bikini bottoms fingering her at the same time, thinking, and commenting that they were used to being stared at, he then carried on massaging Megan's body head to foot in sun cream concentrating on her smooth turnips the most making her nipples stick out harder.

Megan mentioned. "I am enjoying massaging the sun cream onto your skin!"

Vinny had red cheeks. "I am enjoying it as well when you put your hands down my swimming shorts!"

Megan mentioned. "I have pulled them off, releasing your six-inch love thermometer, I am trying not to sit on it with what happened earlier!"

Vinny mentioned. "I need to have a minute apart, or I will shove my baby maker into your love tunnel, the penis is the lightest thing in the world, even a thought can raise it!"

Megan mentioned. "You get worse with your silly comments and jokes!"

Vinny announced. "I know I can't help it, look at the old couple, the gentleman's penis is fully erected with the lady sitting looking at it, she is touching it, I feel proud that we have helped an old couple to enjoy each other!"

Megan agreed. "I am happy for them as well, I

am going to walk into the calm sea to wash the loose sand from me, when a couple gets married the trouble starts when a man and a woman become one, and the main trouble starts when they decide which one."

Vinny just laughed.

Megan walked into the sea, noticing that the same couple were still on the floats with her watching them, with them playing with each others' bodies and kissing passionately.

Vinny walked remarkably close behind her with his sex lollipop still hard as a rock.

Megan walked into the sea slightly. "This lovely light blue sea feels nice and refreshingly cool!"

Vinny stared at the sea. "I have never seen a float as big!"

Megan sounded happy. "I wish that we could join in, I really do think that it is Casey on top of Ghianu."

Vinny agreed. "I think that you are right, she is now sucking his seven-inch fat sperm rod with him shouting with enjoyment, this is turning me on even more!"

Megan asked. "Did you hear him just say oh that is lush, Casey?"

Vinny remarked. "Yes, we definitely know that it is Casey and Ghianu!"

Megan suggested. "At least there is no gritty sand in the water, but there is still salty water that does not taste very nice."

Megan and Vinny swam up to them.

Vinny introduced himself. "Hi Ghianu and Casey, it is nice to see you both again, you have both got plenty of common-sense enjoying sex together where you can wash yourselves as needed!"

Ghianu looked and sounded surprised. "It is nice to see you both together again!"

Megan sounded very giddy. "It is nice to be back

together as a group, are you both still working with the circus?"

Casey glowed with happiness. "Yes, we are, and I am glad that you love each other as much as we do with you both looking cosy on the beach earlier!"

Megan changed the subject. "I really like your mirrored multi-coloured sunglasses and white baseball hats with a small solar-panelled fan in them that you are both wearing to protect yourselves from the hot, scorching sun."

Ghianu laughed. "We call them fanny hats with them having solar fans on them to keep us cool!"

Casey handed Megan and Vinny a fanny hat free of charge each that they had spare on the inflatables.

Vinny was grateful. "I love my free fanny hat, thank you."

Ghianu and Casey explained that they sold the

fanny hats and the
sunglasses for extra money
when they were not working
with the circus people.

Megan sounded
grateful. "Thank you, it will
protect us from the sun!"

Casey felt helpless.
"You're welcome, I would
love you to come and see us
working one day, we love
living permanently around
the corner with the circus
crowd, it is fun!"

Vinny felt
overwhelmed. "It is

definitely really nice us being back together as a gang for us to catch up with each other again, our school days seem so long ago!"

Casey asked. "Do you both want to join us to have a foursome?"

Megan asked. "Why not?"

They started to touch and kiss each other.

There was a small crowd of people watching them by now, including a

police officer in between
playing football with a
beach ball on the soft hot
sand.

Ghianu noticed. "I
have just been watching
them kicking a ball to each
other with sand flying into
the air just missing their
eyes, I think that they are
lucky that it is not getting
kicked anywhere near to
their male reproductive
systems, I feel glad that they
are not hurt by the ball as
yet."

Vinny pulled a scrunched-up face. "I wouldn't want to think about how much pain that would cause, I don't blame them for being careful, it would really hurt if it hit them in their bollocks and it would probably make them cry!"

Megan announced. "I have removed my bikini bottoms under the water, and I have thrown them into the middle of the float, I found it a little difficult to climb onto it, but I feel happy that I did not fall off!"

Vinny asked Megan. "Please pass me your bikini bottoms, I will put them on to the towel to dry!"

Megan replied. "Here and thank you."

Vinny smiled. "I would do anything for you; I will not be long."

Casey muttered softly. "How sweet of him!"

Vinny walked back through the shallow clear sea, then walked onto the burning sand with him shouting. "Ouch." On his way to his towel with his feet getting scalded with every step.

The audience watched every move that he made, with his knob starting to flop about between his legs with him throwing Megan's bikini bottoms onto her towel on the hot sand, he then walked back to the floats arriving back with Megan.

Megan sounded pleasured. "I hope that you don't mind, but I am fingering Casey's hot box!"

Casey announced. "I am fingering Megan's vertical smile at the same time!"

Ghianu raised his voice. "I am enjoying kissing both of them in between them kissing each other."

Vinny sounded a little disappointed. "It sounds

like you have been having fun while I burnt my feet on the sand!"

Ghianu asked Vinny. "Would you like to swap partners for a while?"

He expected a smack in the face for kissing Megan.

Vinny immediately replied. "We are old friends, and I would love to have sex with Casey."

Chapter Eight

They swapped partners

Vinny climbed onto the inflatable with Ghianu, Megan, and Casey.

Ghianu announced. "With Vinny's permission, I am willingly going to push my seven-inch penis into your clit Megan just a little bit and tease you in between a deep thrust, making you scream with joy and pleasure so that you beg for it to go inside of you deeper!"

The crowd of people on the beach looked like they were discussing what they would do next, pointing at them, making them feel like they were on a stage.

Vinny announced. "I am going to slip my just over six-inch dick into you Casey; I will push in so hard; it will make your eyes water!"

Casey looked so glowingly happy with her kissing Vinny at the same time.

They both removed their knobs, then gently and passionately licked and massaged each other from head to foot.

Vinny expressed his opinion assertively. "I really want Megan back!"

They swapped back with Vinny, sucking Megan's tits erotically, while Megan massaged Vinny's poking stick with her soft warm hands.

Casey and Ghianu were kissing with Ghianu,

teasing her pussy with his warm moist tool.

Megan insisted. "Vinny, please put your large pecker into my deep hole!"

Vinny agreed. "I will do that right now!"

Megan asked. "Ghianu, do you want to enter your penis into my anus at the same time while Vinny is in my clit, so that I know what it feels like with a penis inside the back and front of me?"

Ghianu mentioned. "I would love to do that for you, but what about Casey?"

Casey mentioned. "I don't mind watching, then they can do the same to me!"

They all agreed, with Vinny slowly entering Megan's doughnut hole and Ghianu vigorously entered Megan's anus with his hot rod.

Casey sat touching
them all at the side while
fingering herself.

After a good two to
three minutes, Vinny and
Ghianu swapped over to
Casey.

Ghianu entered
Casey's vagina slowly, while
Vinny entered Casey's anus
gently.

Megan lay watching for
a few minutes, enjoying
watching, and felt a little
out of breath touching and
tickling them all gently.

They swapped back to their partners trying not to eject their sperm, but they both announced that they could not hold it in any longer sharing it with them up their pussies, with them expressing their opinion on how amazing the penetration felt of the cum shooting inside of them, explaining that it felt like a gentle flowing feeling filling them.

They gently swam back to their towels for a drink and a rest with Ghianu and

Casey joining them, with them all getting a few drinks each with people walking up to them saying how much they had enjoyed their water float show, with them saying that they were glad that they had enjoyed it.

Vinny and Megan explained to people how they had just met again after losing touch, and they were happy to be back together talking about old times and how they had all met up again, with more people gathering around them saying how amazing it looked.

They all had too much to drink with them, cuddling and kissing random people, including the old couple with the man selling the drinks putting some upbeat Spanish music on loud.

Megan sounded happy. "I am loving everybody dancing together to the music and enjoying themselves!"

Vinny looked around. "Some people are enjoying sex to the beat of the music, shouting to each other instead of talking normally with it being so loud with us not being able to hear each other properly."

Megan smiled. "The old couple are joining in dancing too!"

Vinny smiled. "With us all getting covered in the sand, I want to wash it off."

Megan looked around. "Some people aren't that

bothered about the sand because they are very drunk!"

Vinny pointed out. "Some people have started to dance into the sea with a line of people following each other dancing with one another!"

Megan was fancied the most with how pretty and slim she looked, all of the men wanted to touch Megan's breasts with them having a lot of fans wanting more from them, with them deciding to go live on social

media showing the world
them enjoying erotic loving
sex together.

Vinny got a special
illumines bag for his phone
from the person selling the
drinks that was waterproof
so that he could take photos
in the water.

Vinny started to record
them all on his phone
having sex in the water
showing it live on view time
that people post anything
and everything on with a
million views as soon as he
had turned the camera on

recording, they had too many comments to reply to.

Vinny and Megan wanted a rest from the publicity to spend more time together, stopping going live temporarily filming on view time, discussing that they loved being popular.

They suddenly had people knocking at the door asking for more sex antics for them to watch from them, with them replying that there would be plenty

more coming soon from them.

Chapter Nine

Save the Queen

Vinny asked. "I need you to help me with something!"

Megan asked. "What do you need help with?"

Vinny pointed at an extra-large tent in his large lounge cupboard. "This large door tent that I have bought from a shop in town that was shutting down a while ago, I was hoping to use it in the near future with enough room for twenty people or more inside, I had to get a taxi to transport it home and a lot of my neighbours helped me to carry it inside!"

Megan suggested. "Let's knock on the neighbours' doors so that they can help us set up the tent for a sex party down at the beach in the tent!"

They got many neighbours involved in transporting the tent down to the beach struggling to carry it with a lot of help, setting it up near to the bar, and then advertised on view time that they would be having sex parties inside and outside of the tent on Bloom beach, and explained that all were welcome to join them.

Vinny set up a large photo studio inside of the tent with it turning into a major big sex party, with people from all over the world posing for the camera to show the world them having plenty of foreplay and sex.

Megan bought plenty of boxes of sex items from where she worked with a large discount that she had ordered in bulk including condoms, ladies protective barrier items to stop pregnancies, the morning-after pills, baby oil, massage oils, vibrators, dildos, rampant rabbits, cock rings, anal toys, male masterbators bondage toys and handcuffs to sell them in the tent on the beach at the sex parties.

Megan spoke. "Well, it is our first party selling the sex items in the tent on the beach, and we are making a fortune!"

Vinny organised many more parties and gave up his job because they were so popular and in so much demand and Megan cut her work down to one day a week, with Ghianu and Casey being assistants to Megan and Vinny, with many people attending Bloom Beach from all over the world keeping them constantly busy.

They discussed that it would be a good idea to enter the Ginny book of world records for the biggest sex party in the world on a beach, with them advertising the main biggest sex party ever on a beach for in a weeks time putting the information onto social media and view time.

Vinny spoke. "Which day is best to go to the beach?"

Megan quizzed. "Go on, what is the answer?"

Vinny replied. "Sunday."

Megan laughed. "Very funny, that is so true though!"

John and Margarita appeared at the beach looking at them with a shocked look with them being naked and not knowing where to look, with Margarita announcing that their new home was ready to move into and their items and furniture were on the way to their new home from large storage units, with them thanking Megan for letting them stay, explaining that they would see them

soon, just before they had
left they said that they had
seen them on view time,
they walked off saying that
it was okay if that was what
they wanted to do with an
embarrassing laugh.

The world attended
including the hospital staff
laughing with them at what
had happened earlier and
Carol and Colin, and all of
the people from the pub
earlier with everybody
stripping off licking each
other out or sucking each
other off in the sink with
one another, with them

being filmed by the
television crew, with plenty
of alcohol flowing and loud
music playing keeping
people singing or dancing
along to the beat.

A group of teenagers
announced that they were
going to play a game called
Save the Queen, they
started the game by taking
turns by putting a coin with
the Queen on it into each
others drinks, with
everybody saying 'Save the
Queen' on repeat until they
had drank the drink
making them drink faster,

making them get more
drunk, then that person that
had just had the coin in
their drink, then that
person does the same to
another person, with people
in the group saying 'Save
the Queen' together getting
louder on repeat as they all
get even more drunk.

Megan and Vinny
joined in with Megan
getting two coins in her
drink, making her drink
double fast, with people
laughing and shouting.
"Save the Queen." Until the
glass was empty, she then

put the coins into Vinny's drink with him drinking amazingly fast as well, with Vinny passing the coins around the table a few times.

Everybody discussed how they would like to climb onto the inflatables in the sea and organise a race, with whoever gets there first has got the choice of who they want sex with, with them racing into the sea with Megan arriving at the floats first obviously choosing Vinny with everyone else climbing onto the floats enjoying foreplay with one another and sex together, with people touching each others bodies erotically with desperation for each other.

Megan asked. "Please swim back to the tent with me, Vinny to join the people left behind still drinking inside of the tent!"

They raced back, with Vinny winning the race back to shore, with him buying them some drinks to celebrate him winning the race.

Chapter Ten

Newspaper journalists could not stop taking photos

The camera operator was standing inside of the tent complaining that he could not film everybody at the same time.

Ghianu and Casey started to record people also from different angles broadcasting live on to view time, having fun as well as recording people doing different daring sex positions.

The photographer asked everybody over a microphone to spray their cum into the air if they could so that he, Ghianu and Casey could get some amazing photos of the cum flying into the air, it was like there were hundreds of creamy sticky fireworks going off at the same time.

Megan and Vinny could just see a sea of bodies touching, teasing, kissing, and having sex with many enjoyable noises coming from different people, with them overhearing a couple with the man saying that he would cunnilingus her.

Megan commented. "That sounds different."

The man explained. "It means that I enjoy licking wet and inviting pussy and it is a Latin word!"

Vinny spoke. "Why is a pussy like a grapefruit?"

Megan replied. "What is the answer?"

Vinny answered. "The best one's squirt when you suck them."

Megan laughed. "Very funny."

Vinny smiled. "It is nice us laid at the side of each other on this towel, I am going to lick your hole out, then I will lick you from head to foot!"

Megan sounded graceful. "I am loving touching you tenderly everywhere, please put your cock in between my tits for a while, then put your cock up my middle flower hole and move in and out fast then spurt your cum up inside of me like nectar from a bee!"

Vinny looked hot. "I am feeling very hot, I am really enjoying it in between your tits, I am moving into your clit now, I can't hold it back any longer, I am ejaculating inside of your clit in a second."

Megan suggested. "I am hot too, I think that we need to rest for a while, look at the crowd of people on the inflatables full of people, anybody can see that everybody is enjoying each others naked bodies!"

Vinny's eyes nearly popped out of his sockets. "Yes, it is an amazing, unbelievable sight to see that we have created, I am proud of us!"

A few hours went by with them sunbathing, with Megan and Vinny starting to touch one another again.

Megan smiled. "That didn't take very long for the cameraman suddenly appearing on us!"

Vinny expressed his opinion. "It didn't no, but I don't mind, I am loving you sucking my cock, it feels electric!"

Megan announced. "I am enjoying sucking it."

Vinny sounded panicked. "You need to stop for a while because I am going to cum in a minute, I will lick your jugs while I pour sweet wine onto your hole!"

Everybody around them were watching them.

Ghianu and Casey joined in with Megan and Vinny, with Ghianu stroking between Megan's legs softly, with Vinny stroking between Casey's legs with their bellends, with them both wet through, announcing that they wanted their long fat cocks inside of them.

Megan grabbed hold of Ghianu's pleasure rider sucking it hard, with Casey doing the same to Vinny, with Vinny licking all of the sweet wine from Megan's clit, with her eyes shut enjoying it so much with a big smile on her face, with Vinny moving into Megan's clit moving in and out hard, with Ghianu doing the same to Casey, with them exploding every bit up into them with them out of breath talking about how there was not much room left on the beach for people to sit, or lay down with

everybody enjoying one
another.

The world was
watching everybody on the
beach and in the sea having
the biggest sex party that
you have ever seen, with
everybody feeling happy
making patterns in the sand
with their bodies, feet, and
hands with them also going
into the sea.

There were sticky cum
flying into the air
everywhere all over each
other with a few people that
had not stripped off but

were just watching and recording onto social media and live on view time through their phones, more people arrived at the available pockets of sand that were spare, people started having foursomes with each other, with the whole beach touching and having sex with one another, with the sea and the floats full also, with many people in a queue to enter onto the floats in the sea.

Megan and Vinny discussed going to Vinny's

home for a sleep and walk there together hand in hand, after a sleep holding each other, they had a shower together washing each other, they then walked back down to Bloom Beach.

People walked up to Vinny and Megan thanking them for making this opportunity for them saying that it was the most fun that they had ever had in their lives, with the music getting louder with everybody dancing until the early hours of the morning, with the cameraman leaving and people started to leave slowly, struggling to put their clothes back on with them having one too many drinks staggering back to their homes, or hotels.

Megan spoke. "We have sold lots of sex toys; this makes me feel happy with us making lots of money and making other people happy for using them!"

Vinny smiled. "It makes me feel happy too, I will turn the music off, then shut and padlock the zip on the tent, we can then walk back to my home to go to bed!"

As Vinny woke the next morning, he gently woke Megan with his warm hard dick touching her in the back, with him still being a little half-asleep licking Megan's clit with her making noises like. 'Uh,' and 'Ooh' and more random noises, with him massaging her body with his fingers at the same time making her move around with joy from him gently

tickling her body, he then
stuck his hot rod up her clit
moving in and out fast, with
her stroking Vinny's body
gently in between his heavy
thrusts pulling his bottom
towards her, with Vinny
announcing that he could
not hold back any longer
ejaculating his cum up
inside of her.

They got washed and
dressed then went back
down to the beach, the
journalists from the
newspapers came to take
plenty of photos with Vinny,
Megan, Ghianu and Casey

because they had won the Ginny book of World Records for the most people on a beach having sex at the same time.

Casey announced. "I think that we are all proud of ourselves for winning!"

A journalist spoke. "We might as well remove our clothes and find someone with no partner or join in with others and have sex with everybody in the sea and take photos of ourselves at the same time

with our waterproof
cameras!"

Ghianu sounded
grateful. "I love it how the
fish massage people's feet
and eat the dead skin, I am
really enjoying you giving
me a blow job Casey!"

Vinny announced. "I
will lick you out for a while,
Megan, then we can enjoy a
foursome again with more
sex on the floats in the sea!"

Chapter Eleven

Hotel parties

One of the journalists had dropped their camera into the shallow warm clear sea with Casey swimming down to the bottom of the sand to pick the camera up, with the journalist thanking Casey for fetching the camera for him from under the water, with Casey saying you're welcome back, she then went back to enjoying sucking all of the different dicks, with plenty of volunteers to help out sucking them with her.

Megan, Vinny, Ghianu and Casey discussed setting up sex boat rides, with the tent on the beach doing very well making them money with them thinking of different ways to expand the business ordering plenty of boats, with them dressing the boats with soft pillows and blankets for people to enjoy sex on, with complimentary sex toys dotted around with some having slow and some having fast music playing on each of the boats, they started ringing around and buying what they needed.

Casey and Ghianu were in charge of the naked sex boat rides on the water, with the boat rides being so popular that they had to employ a lot of people making a franchise all over the world called 'Shenanigans on the Sea boat rides,' with them making more money than they had expected, with the staff constantly cleaning all of the cum up from all over the boats to stop people slipping.

Vinny spoke to Megan." I just want a holiday away with you and I have decided that we are going to a really nice posh hotel!"

Megan sounded ecstatic. "That would be great, let's just get a few items from our homes on the way!"

As they arrived, they enjoyed a top-class meal in the restaurant all dressed up, as soon as they had finished, they walked upstairs into the bedroom stripping each other's clothes off.

Vinny grinned. "I am tying you to the bed with a pair of handcuffs out of your bag from earlier for a bit of fun, is that okay?"

Megan smirked, laughing. "That is fine with me, go ahead but just lock one hand up for now so that I can move more freely to give you pleasure as well, I am pouring a yoghurt over your knob from the dining room that I had put in my bag earlier and I will lick it off enjoying every second!"

Vinny begged. "Please get on top of my dick and bounce up and down on it with your tits bouncing up and down on my chest, being careful not to hurt yourself with the handcuff!"

Megan screamed. "I have been bouncing a while now, I fancy a change, please put the other handcuff on my other hand and whip me for a while with the whip that I put in my bag for us both to get pleasure out of it!"

Vinny sounded excited. "I will put the other handcuff on and whip you now!"

Megan sounded grateful. "This feels good, you can now fuck me in my arse until you ejaculate inside of me!"

Vinny announced. "I am getting to my climax, are you?"

Megan agreed. "Yes, I am, it looks like we are both coming at the same time!"

Vinny asked. "Do you want me to move into your clit for a while and spurt up there instead?"

Megan asked. "If you want!"

Vinny sounded out of breath. "You feel so nice, I am ejaculating inside of you now!"

Megan asked. "It was a little awkward with the handcuffs on, will you please let me free from the handcuffs now so that we can have a shower together?"

Vinny announced, catching his breath back. "I will look for the handcuff key from your bag now, I have looked all through your bag, and I can't find it, I will empty your bag onto the floor!"

Megan sounded panicked. "I can't see the key anywhere, what are we going to do?"

Vinny laughed. "Oh dear, I will have to phone the fire brigade because that is the only way that you are going to be free, I hope that you don't need to go to the toilet desperately for a while!"

All of the staff and customers in the hotel thought that their room was on fire at first with the firefighters arriving at their door, until they had found out what had really happened with them in hysterics of laughter, with the firefighters walking into Megan and Vinny's room.

A firefighter announced. "We are your biggest fans on view time, we feel proud that we have released you from the bed!"

Vinny agreed. "I am pleased that Megan is free too!"

The firefighter laughed, announcing. "We will see you both down at the beach soon, bye!"

The firefighters were laughing on the way out.

Megan and Vinny left
the room to go down to the
beach and got into the lift
with a man in the lift saying.
"I speak Spanish polla."

Laughing on the way
down with Megan asking
loudly what it meant.

The man explained that
it meant 'Dick.'

Laughing while
walking off, Megan laughed
as well.

Vinny suggested. "Let's
go to different nudist
beaches and make love!"

Megan agreed. "Yes, we will later, let's go to my house for a rest first!"

Vinny sounded happy. "I feel proud of us because we are making it onto every talk, sex, and other programs on the television after nine at night with us known as the sex-mad couple!"

Megan suggested. "Let's go to the chocolate festival next door instead!"

Vinny grabbed Megan's hand. "Come on then, let's go, I can feel eyes on us and smiling faces looking at us as we walk!"

Megan mentioned. "This is what they are all waiting for, us kissing each other and stripping on the television, ripping each others clothes off!"

Vinny announced. "I will buy a large jar of runny chocolate and pour it all over your tits so that I can lick and suck it all off with enjoyment for us both!"

Megan sounded incredibly happy. "Your

tongue feels so nice and warm on my tits!"

Vinny suggested. "We can lay down on that blanket, then you can sit on my warm stick with it being hard as a rock!"

They rolled over onto each other on the soft blanket on the floor with the crowd of people starting to join in having sex together, with the chocolate workers saying that it was their best day that they had ever had at work in their life.

Megan sounded jolly. "That felt so good, we both spurted our cum together in sync with each other!"

Vinny sounded surprised. "Yes, we must be able to read each other when we are ejaculating, I feel even more proud of us with every television show wanting us on their show."

Megan announced. "All of the shows have got to be on after nine at night with us finding it hard to keep our raunchy sexual needs under control!"

Vinny mentioned. "I have lost count of how many invitations to different parties me, you, Ghianu, and Casey constantly get invited to!"

Megan sounded proud. "I know we are celebrities now; I have always wanted to go to a country called Pat-grass, let's get on our private plane now to find different beaches with our faces on the billboard!"

Vinny replied. "Ok, let's go."

Megan suggested. "We just need to get a taxi to the nearest nudist beach and find the billboard on the entrance with ours, and Ghianu and Casey's names and faces on it, so that we can take some photos and then we can chill out for a while!"

Vinny sounded touched. "I feel welcome here and it is a nice beach with so many people welcoming us with open arms!"

Megan and Vinny apologised that Ghianu and Casey were not with them at that moment in time and explained that they would visit Pat-grass another time in the near future, but they could take lots of photos of them for now.

Megan felt wanted in a loving way. "This is a very welcoming beach; I am going to enjoy stripping you Vinny now that we are comfy!"

They removed each other's clothes quickly, with

Megan laying down on her towel.

Vinny sounded happy. "I am enjoying licking your gorgeous body, Megan, from top to bottom!"

Megan teased. "I am enjoying teasing you with my fingers on your body, you feel so soft, in a few minutes, I will suck your magic wand!"

Vinny spoke softly. "You make my skin feel lovely and tingly, and my cock feel so hard."

Megan announced. "I will stop sucking your dick in a minute and cuddle you for a while because I love the feel of your body against mine!"

Vinny looked around. "Look around us, everyone else is doing the same, it is like they are learning what to do from us!"

Megan agreed. "Yes, you are right, it is a pleasant feeling!"

Vinny announced. "I am going to stick my sperm poker into your warm, moist love hole!"

Megan sounded pleased. "You are making my pussy spurt everywhere with you moving in and out that fast!"

Vinny looked warm in the cheeks. "I am shooting my cum up inside of you now as well to add to your pussy juices!"

Megan announced. "I can see that we both feel

even happier now with a massive smile on both of our faces!"

Vinny suggested. "Let's have a little sleep for a while, then travel back home to Toke!"

They slept for a short while.

Megan and Vinny woke hours later.

Megan looked in deep thought. "I have got a bright idea; we could set up our own learn-how-to-have-sex school on the beach!"

Vinny's eyes lit up. "That is a good idea, let's get Ghianu and Casey involved and set it up now!"

Ghianu announced. "I have just set the website up, and we are sold out already, we don't need to advertise because there are queues of people on the waiting list already!"

Casey suggested. "We need to employ more people, but only people that know what they are doing with plenty of sex experience that would love every minute teaching couples how to get extra steamy together under the covers!"

Megan sounded pleased. "I am glad that it has got an excellent start to our business!"

Vinny laughed. "How do construction workers party?"

Megan asked. "What is the answer?"

Vinny answered. "They raise the roof."

Megan laughed. "You are funny."

Chapter Twelve

Shenanigans holidays

Vinny smiled. "Our tent is like an intense sex club; we need to put a tent on every nudist beach all over the world!"

Megan agreed. "You are right, let's get that organised now and welcome everyone inside with every background from shy people to people that have never had sex before and more."

Vinny looked shocked. "There are people on the website requesting if they could volunteer their sex help!"

Casey suggested. "Yes, the volunteers can help to get a sex tent in every country in the world up and running!"

Ghianu suggested. "I think that we should set up our own nudist all-inclusive holidays up!"

Megan demanded. "I think that we should do that now!"

Vinny sounded ecstatic. "I think that we are the biggest employers in the world at the moment!"

Casey sounded jolly. "It is nice to be popular!"

Ghianu announced happily. "We have taken loads of cash; I think that we are also the richest people in the world at the moment!"

Megan sounded incredibly happy. "That is a nice feeling for a change!"

Vinny mentioned. "We need our own special nudist planes that are especially for our own holidaymakers, we should call our new company shenanigans on the beach holidays!"

Megan announced. "As soon as it is on the website, it will sell out, I am one hundred percent sure about that!"

Ghianu announced happily. "We have got thousands of bookings already, you were correct!"

Casey suggested. "We just need plane staff that are naked, but we have got plenty of volunteers willing to work for us to touch customers on the way past, so that isn't a problem."

Vinny happily announced. "I think that our new staff will be welcoming the passengers to finger them or tug them off on their way past while they are serving cold drinks only."

Ghianu's eyes were open wide. "The volunteers waiting list is so big!"

Megan suggested. "I think that we should have a rule that the staff that work on the planes only strip their clothes off as the planes have taken off, then get dressed just before they land!"

Ghianu mentioned. "There are that many people that are booking at the same time as soon as shenanigans on the beach holidays went live, the website temporarily stopped working because I think too many people were trying to book their unique sexy holiday that they can't get anywhere else at the same time!"

Megan mentioned. "That is good that a lot of people are still booking with us!"

Casey announced. "We have got many excellent reviews on the website saying that staff that work in our hotels have joined in stripping naked with the visitors!"

Megan stared at the reviews on her phone. "I have just read a review saying that some staff have put a name badge-sized sign around their necks making it clear if guests are welcome to touch them or not, I think that is a good idea!"

Vinny announced. "I have just read another review saying that people are enjoying sex in the swimming pools, or at the side of the pool, at the bar, or anywhere that they wanted to have sex!"

Megan smiled with a gleaming grin. "I am glad that people are enjoying our hotels!"

Ghianu suggested. "We need to organise many sex trips and excursions away from the hotel!"

Casey announced. "We can organise that, people

can strip off when they get
to the private venue!"

Vinny announced. "I
have sent an email to our
staff to organise that, we
need to get in that taxi now
for our own closed-off
private party for just us and
a few selected guests, please,
get a few clothes on
temporarily!"

Ghianu mentioned.
"That journey didn't take
very long, we have arrived
at our private bowling
party, everybody strip off

and release your body parts
freely!"

They stripped.

Vinny suggested. "I
will bowl my ball down the
bowling alley first!"

A guest in their private
bowling party decided that
it would be an excellent idea
to try to put his cock inside
of the holes of one of the
bowling balls to see if it
fitted inside.

Megan shouted at him.
"What are you doing?"

The guest had a sheepish smile. "I wanted to know what it would feel like putting my knob inside, but it is stuck inside where my fingers were supposed to go!"

Megan mentioned. "I can see, that is so funny!"

When everybody had nearly stopped laughing so hard at his stupidity, Megan phoned the fire brigade and the ambulance.

Casey mentioned. "I suppose we had all better get dressed again apart from you with your cock stuck in the hole of the bowling ball!"

Ghianu laughed. "Why shouldn't you play basketball with a pig?"

Vinny asked. What is the answer?"

Ghianu answered. "Because he hogs the ball."

Megan laughed. "Very funny, the emergency services are here!"

The man cried in pain with the ball squashing his cock.

Vinny recognised that they were the same crew that had attended and had helped them before, with them laughing taking the man away and laughing out of the door commenting that the ball may need cutting from him while struggling to carry him, with the ball making his knob stretch a little.

The man sounded concerned. "I hope that you do not cut my knob off!"

They stripped each other's clothes off again as the emergency services had left the building, with it being Megan's turn to bowl next.

Casey sounded concerned. "Be careful when you bend over Megan because your tits look top-heavy!"

Megan agreed. "You are right, my massive breasts have made me fall down the bowling alley, pulling me over onto the floor!"

Many people were offering to pick Megan up from the floor.

Vinny sounded caring. "I will pick you up, grab my hand and skip the game for your own safety; I will play with you instead; I will kiss your tits better first, then

move onto every other part
of your body!"

Everybody could not
take their eyes off them.

Megan kissed Vinny. "I
love kissing you Vinny, your
lips are so soft and smooth!"

Vinny stroked Megan's
arm. "I love kissing you
back and teasing you and
pushing my cock in slightly
like this."

Megan begged. "I am
begging for you to put it all
of the way inside!"

Vinny stroked Megan's bottom. "I love your warm moist vagina and when you pull my bottom towards you, making it finally go all of the way up inside of your lovely and warm hole, it is amazing, it's like a dream."

Megan sounded disappointed slightly. "I am not as keen when you pull your cock out like now teasing me!"

Vinny stroked Megan's hair. "I like a change, like now, I am pulling it out, then shoving it into your mouth, are you loving the flavour of your juices on my cock?"

Megan agreed. "You're right, I love everything that we do, put your young man into my ass for a while!"

Vinny was making enjoyable noises. "This feels so good, your ass is so soft and tight, I love moving in and out, how does it feel with me fingering you at the same time?"

Megan screamed." It feels amazing, carry-on."

Vinny smiled. "I will move my cock back inside of your pussy and shag you hard, I think that we are both coming to our crowning point!"

There was a big audience watching as they were about to cum together with sweat dripping from them.

The audience were turned on near them touching each other, having foreplay and sex, with Megan screaming with joy as he ejaculated his warm welcoming cum into Megan, with her happy, smiling face saying how much she had enjoyed it.

There was a sea of bodies having sex with cum flying into the air and onto peoples' bodies.

Megan and Vinny got dressed, they then walked back to the hotel having a rest for a few hours, they then travelled back to Bloom Beach with it still full of nude people enjoying sex, with some people still just coming to take photos and share them on view time, with Megan and Vinny sharing their opinion that they had set off a trend with everybody enjoying sex with the curtains open in their homes as well to make their lives more exciting.

Chapter Thirteen

The cigarette set the parachute on fire in the air

Megan and Vinny travelled around all of the City with them feeling so welcome everywhere that they went, with them getting invited into houses, shops, workplaces and many more different places, as they entered most places there was cum flying about all around the room covering one another in it, with one group of office staff inviting Megan and Vinny to a naked skydive with the chocolate factory workers that they had already visited joining in as well, with Vinny and Megan jumping at the chance of this, they were just worried about the public and what the police would say with them being naked.

The skydive day came, and they were all strapped up ready to go strapped to another person if that is what they wanted so that they could have sex in the air with the television cameras there to see if they got into the 'Ginny book of world records,' with them attempting to take a few clean photos with Megan, and Vinny starting the skydive off going first off the cliff with them saying that they felt a little frightened with how high up they were, with Megan holding onto Vinny tight around his waist, even though she was strapped in with her knockers bouncing around onto Vinny's back, he commented how nice it felt with Megan jerking him off.

A person in the gang decided to light a cigarette just before setting off into the air, as he left the side of the cliff his parachute burst into flames with him throwing his cigarette to the floor, with another naked lady parachute member flying towards him with him grabbing hold of her, clipping one clip onto one half of her parachute, with him sticking his dick inside of her back passage with her enjoying every second with him holding onto her for dear life while they floated down together landing in the sea, with him panicking because he could not swim very good, with the lifeboat arriving to pick them up out of the sea, they started to travel back to dry land with the lifeboat workers not being able to stop laughing at them in between chatting to them asking if they were okay?

As the couple got to dry land, they shared saying that they were okay now that they were out of the sea saying how amazing it was, and it was a different jump that they both did not expect, realising that they had just cracked a joke without realising it laughing, with the couple announcing that they liked each other, and they swapped telephone numbers.

A police officer walked up to him, arresting him for indecent exposure for having sex in the air and dropping his cigarette to the floor because it could have set the grass on fire if it had landed on the grass with it polluting the sea instead.

The lady shared that she was going to the police station with him, with them being given some clothes that they had found lying about on a shelf in a room full of lost property items that were far too big for them, they could hear people laughing and talking about them in the next room, putting the clothes on anyway, feeling a little bit like idiots with them being the talk of the police station, with the two policemen trying to hold their laughter back questioning them.

The lady crawled
under the table in front of
the policemen giving them a
free blow job each with the
police releasing them with
no charge because they did
not want the strange gossip
to get out about them
getting an unexpected blow
job that should not have
happened, a police colleague
that was with the police
officer that had arrested
them called him a bit of a
jobs worth, with them
agreeing with him.

The couple kept in
touch talking about their

experiences skydiving to new people that they met in the future as a talking point, giving them advice to not skydive and smoke at the same time laughing every time he told people, saying that they have been there, done that, and they have got the T-shirt with embarrassing results.

Vinny opened a letter that had arrived at her home commenting to Vinny, "We are going to be in the Ginny book of world records for our naked skydive!"

Vinny replied. "That is amazing, let's go and tell Ghianu and Casey and enjoy a game of tennis together sharing the good news with them on Bloom nudist beach!"

Megan suggested. "Let's go now."

They arrived and enjoyed the game together sharing the good news, with Megan's massive tits bouncing up and down like mad, with a crowd loving watching their game while they were glued to Megan's breasts with their eyes, with them discussing how Ghianu and Casey were as famous as Vinny and Megan everywhere that they went finishing the game, they then went home afterwards.

Vinny booked an adult-only hotel room in one of his own hotels, making it a special atmosphere with dimmed lights, petals, champagne, chocolates, and a special meal with him getting down on one knee on the balcony.

Megan asked. "What are you doing?"

Vinny asked emotionally. "Will you marry me?"

Vinny pulled a sparkly diamond ring out of a ring box from his pocket.

Megan cried. "Yes, I would love to marry you, I didn't even have to think about it!"

They both had an amazing smile on their

faces, with them immediately planning their wedding, ordering her white dress that clings to her tiny waist, announcing that it is on view time that all were welcome to attend.

On the run-up to the wedding, the preparations for everything got underway with the hotel staff organising everything for them that he had chosen with everything running perfectly smooth, with them getting married in the main hall of the hotel, with lots of congratulations, claps and confetti being thrown over them.

The large wedding party then followed Megan and Vinny down to the large dining room for their meal and speech, with nearly all of the world attending the wedding, with Ghianu being the best man, and Casey was the bridesmaid with the speech mainly about all of the amazing times that they had enjoyed with the highs and lows that had happened recently and in the past, with everybody having a free sex toy on their table each to enjoy using, with everybody discussing that they could not wait to use it asking Megan and Vinny to join in with them using their complimentary items.

Megan said that it was their hotel and if she wanted a sex session at her wedding she would, lifting her white long floaty dress that went to just below her knees up above her head, showing that she had no underwear on with everybody else joining in as they had finished eating.

Vinny laughed. "I think that it is most probably a first with the bride flashing people!"

People discussed that they wished that it could go into the Ginny book of world records with all of the wedding party having sex, with people looking through the windows enjoying every second pointing at all of the different people enjoying sex using all of the different sex items provided.

Megan unzipped Vinny's trousers letting his

knob out, with her gently touching Vinny's penis moving her hand up and down watching it grow larger, mentioning that their wedding day could not be any more perfect while bending down sucking his penis, with Vinny struggling to unzip Megan's dress with it falling to the floor while Vinny stroked in between her legs, with her cum dripping down them.

Megan glowed. "I am loving sucking your dick hard."

Vinny sounded lovingly happy. "I love it too, let's lay down on the red-carpeted floor and roll about kissing, and cuddling!"

Megan kneeled down on her knees while Vinny pushed his dick up her arse while fingering her at the same time, moving in and out fast, then he moved into her juicy clit with her shouting. "More and faster, please." With him thrusting in and out fast.

Vinny announced. "It is an amazing erotic electric atmosphere with everybody else enjoying sex around us, I am squirting my sperm up inside of you!"

They all got dressed and finished their meals discussing how they enjoyed their sex wedding with a meal and plenty of drinks, they all then went back to get freshened up, and the whole wedding party travelled to the nudist Bloom beach with them to enjoy a sex party together showing their wedding rings

off, with everybody
sampling the boat rides
nearly falling overboard
because they were drunk.

Vinny and Megan said
goodbye to everybody then
travelled on one of their
planes to their sex hotel
with them removing their
clothes to blend in, signing
autographs for people and
they joined in with the hotel
activities which mainly
involved sex, or foreplay,
with them going for a walk
enjoying looking around the
gift shops, looking at all of
the items that they sold

feeling elated, walking upstairs to put some clothes on, they then went out of the hotel for a walk around being recognised by everybody with everyone saying. "Hi."

A small group of males and females walked up to them explaining that they wanted a sex lesson, inviting them inside of their home with them following them inside of their lounge.

Megan and Vinny laid down on the floor next to each other asking them to do the same as them, with them stripping their clothes off, they then started to kiss tenderly while stroking each other at the same time with Vinny stroking Megan's body with his bell end, with Megan lying there enjoying every second, with everybody mirroring what they did, with Megan then sucking Vinny's dick lovingly.

Vinny announced. "I will lick your warm doughnut hole with passion in a minute, Megan, then I will get on top of you and move my dick in and out fast."

Megan looked at her breasts. "I love it when my tits bounce up and down on your chest, they make everyone stare at us even more!"

Vinny announced. "I feel like I am getting to my crowning point!"

Megan screamed with enjoyment with the other couples doing the same looking over at them.

The small group
thanked Megan and Vinny.

Megan and Vinny got
up and had a walk around
with them loving having a
nosy around the lounge,
with them finding their
music system with Megan
putting some music on loud
with them enjoying a party
dancing with them, with
them feeling happy together
while still being naked
chatting loudly, practising
massaging each other all
over with the group of
people saying that they had

never had as much fun with
a few hours passing by.

Megan and Vinny
announced that they felt
tired saying that they were
going, but they would visit
again with them getting
dressed, they then waved
goodbye with the group
thanking them again saying
that they were good
teachers asking how much
they owed for their tuition,
with them saying that it was
free that day, with the
group thanking them for
their kindness, they then

walked back to the hotel with them going to sleep.

Vinny spoke to Megan. "It might be a good idea to set up a cooking sex-making workshop downstairs in the restaurant!"

Megan smiled. "What a good idea."

They walked downstairs naked with the guests joining in making their own knob lollipops and tit buns, with them walking around with them with many more people joining in loving making them with enjoyment discussing how much fun it was making it a regular thing every week, making the lollipops and tits, with them getting many more bookings, as the word got around on social media and view time with how much fun they were having.

Because their customers enjoyed the bun and cock making workshop, Megan decided to set up a workshop in the reception area making a statue together with many volunteers for the outside of the hotel made from paper mache into a large cock with them getting covered in a sticky substance, with them commenting that it looked and felt a little bit like cum, they then painted the cock making it look real with white cream cum spurting out of the top of it, a lot of the customers did not want to stop at making just a cock, they made a large pair of tits as well, placing them in pride and place putting them outside of the hotel door with them looking amazing.

Journalists arrived with them filming and taking photos of Megan and Vinny at the side of the large cock and the pair of tits with everybody that had helped to make them in the background of the photos, with the journalists making their own knob lollipops, then they enjoyed a swim in the pool with the ladies that had volunteered sexual love, sucking them off on an inflatable in the swimming pool with the journalists thanking Gemma and Vinny, saying that they felt

better with their complimentary blow job in the pool, they then left feeling extremely happy.

Chapter Fourteen

Private circus party

Megan and Vinny were sitting at the reception bar chatting with their customers noticing and talking about a man making a cupboard in the reception area from scratch making a lot of noise with his tools, swearing out loud to himself struggling on his own with him dropping all of his screws onto the floor with them scattering about everywhere.

Megan and Vinny
helped him pick the screws
up, trying to avoid standing
on them with the man
asking Megan if she wanted
to help him with him
struggling?

Megan smiled. "Why
not? "

Vinny went back to the
bar to finish his drink.

He asked her to pass
him a screw while staring at
her tits.

Megan helped by passing him items that he needed with her still being naked, with him looking at her like he wanted to kiss her with his lips getting closer to hers, asking her if she needed a screw because he had plenty?

Vinny was still chatting at the bar, enjoying a pint.

Megan replied that she already had plenty in her hand and did not need any more.

The man just looked at her strangely with her

realising that he wanted sex with her, stripping him off and releasing his cock, letting him put his fat long hot poker inside of her hole.

Vinny immediately arrived with them joining in also, touching Megan using some baby oil that he had got from the reception desk, using the baby oil to massage each other, moving on to the comfy cream sofas, sliding about underfoot with some baby oil on the floor in the reception area where they were using it with an audience gathering around

them watching every move
that they made.

The man stroked
Megan's body.

Vinny then stuck his
cock inside of Megan's clit,
moving in and out fast, with
the man jerking himself off
over them both standing
next to them, with the
crowd of people joining in
with them having sex with
each other.

Vinny and Megan
sneaked away to their room,
leaving the people to it,

deciding that the next day
they would travel back to
Bloom Beach.

It was the next day
with them saying how much
they enjoyed their sleep and
eating breakfast, they then
got dressed and travelled
back on the plane and the
rest of the way in the taxi,
as they arrived some people
were complaining because
the morning-after pills did
not work, with them finding
out that they were pregnant
with more people
complaining, with some of

the items that they had sold, they had broken already.

They apologised for them being broken and sorted the problems out with the sex items company Shenanigans and replaced the broken items, giving the unhappy customers a free holiday.

Ghianu and Casey joined them on the beach enjoying each other with Casey and Megan kissing, and Vinny and Ghianu caressed them all over from head to foot undressing each other, they then swam into the sea onto the floats with Megan sucking Vinny off, and Casey sucked Ghianu's dick with them licking them out at the same time while still touching each other, with the men moving into their soft warm vaginas pushing in and out gently trying not to cum straight away, having to keep taking their cocks out moving them near to their holes, while erotically kissing them, with them pushing them back in hard announcing that they were about to squirt up their vaginas, with Casey and Megan's hands on their bottoms keeping their dicks up them with them coming to their crowning point shouting. "Awww yes." Together.

They enjoyed a little swim, they then walked back onto the sand, they then got dressed.

Megan suggested. "Do you want to go to the circus where Ghianu and Casey work?"

Vinny agreed. "Yes, what a good idea!"

As they arrived they joined in with many people practising working on their show routines, with Megan watching a man climbing a rope sharing her thoughts with them with her wondering what it would be like to climb it with Megan stood at the bottom of the rope looking up, with her starting to climb the rope with her not being able to climb it at all.

Vinny had a go at tightrope walking; his legs wobbled so much with him having to get off the rope because he nearly fell off.

Megan and Vinny juggled some balls, dropping them mostly, feeling proud that they had at least had a go at it, with Vinny joking about saying that he was glad that she had not dropped his balls.

Megan had a go on the unicycle enjoying it but felt like she would fall off complaining a little that it

was un-comfy, with no
clothes on.

Megan and Vinny
decided to just say hello to
the audience and promised
not to take their clothes off
with it being the evening of
the performance.

Everybody was so
pleased with Megan and
Vinny being there with
them being swamped at the
end of the performance with
everybody asking for them
to go back to their homes,
hotels, and parties, and they
were asking for their

autographs, with Vinny announcing to the audience that they would be doing an adult only performance the next day with children not allowed to attend that performance, and announced that they would be in the performance with plenty of raunchy items to buy afterwards to spice up their sex lives.

They turned the circus into a private party, getting organised with different things that they could do, the animals that lived there

must have wondered what
was going on.

It was the next day,
and everybody arrived with
not a seat spare in the
audience.

Megan and Vinny
learnt new things from the
circus people and the circus
people learnt new things
from Megan and Vinny,
mainly the best sex
positions.

The circus crew were
on the stage announcing
that Megan and Vinny

would be on the stage soon
with a few more acts.

Megan and Vinny
finally walked onto the
stage.

Megan felt proud. "We
are very happy to be here
on this stage entertaining
you!"

Vinny kissed Megan.
"It is lovely to see so many
smiling faces!"

They started the
performance that they knew
best, stripping off, touching

one another passionately and enjoying each other.

Megan picked up some balls, juggling with her dropping the balls with her not being able to see them properly with her big breasts in the way, giving it up with plenty of laughter coming from the audience.

Megan put Vinny's fire hose into her mouth sucking it with enjoyment with her moving it in and out of her mouth, with Vinny getting onto a unicycle, with Megan trying to still suck his knob as he cycled around, with the audience laughing even louder with Vinny getting off the unicycle, peoples eyes were stuck to them with them nearly crying because they had laughed so much.

Vinny then licked Megan's pussy with her making all kinds of noises from the way that he put his tongue inside with him wiggling it about, with him then moving his warm rod inside of Megan's warm, inviting clit with the audience joining in stripping off getting saucy with the person sat next to them, with everybody copying the same as what they were doing.

Megan shouted. "I hope that you are enjoying yourselves?"

The audience shouted back. "Yes."

Vinny massaged Megan with his dick all over, then pushed back inside of her hole moving in and out vigorously, he then sucked Megan's breasts with enjoyment, with Vinny announcing that he could not hold his cum back any longer ejaculating up inside of her thanking the audience for attending with them all getting dressed.

The audience clapped loudly, they then eventually left their seats, as they had put their clothes back on purchasing many sex items on their way out.

They enjoyed a few drinks of alcohol and then slept on the stage.

The next day they thanked everyone in the circus, they then went back to Megan's home waving goodbye to everybody, with everybody saying how much they had enjoyed themselves with plenty of cum around the room, making the floor slippery.

Carol and Colin appeared with them back from their holiday, congratulating them for their fame and wealth.

Vinny and Megan set up their own sex museum

with plenty of photos on the wall of them in different places with most of the world on Bloom Beach, hotels, the circus, peoples homes, swimming pools and many more places with people bringing old sex items in, donating the items to the museum.

Megan wrote a letter to her work announcing that she was putting in her notice because she did not need to go anymore with her doing well in their own business.

Vinny and Megan were over the moon that they had finally got into the Ginny Book of world records.

Carol and Colin went back to Megan's home with them and enjoyed a private sex session together stripping off in the bedroom, with Megan and Vinny licking, touching, and kissing each other gently, caressing each other tenderly mainly in between their legs, with Carol and Colin doing the same.

Carol and Megan fingered each other while the ladies moved their hands up and down on their dicks.

Vinny suggested. "Let us have a turn at fingering you!"

Colin mentioned. "This makes a pleasant change for us all in your room together, I love your pussy Carol, it is so warm and wet!"

Carol sounded caring. "I love your fingers, they feel amazing!"

Vinny sounded full filled. "I love fingering you, Megan, it is so tight and smooth your clit!"

The men put their sticks inside of their holes with them rolling over on top of each other getting hot and moving in and out, with Megan, and Carol wet through with their cum covering the bed, with Vinny and Ghianu announcing that they were about to explode erupting their cum inside of them.

Megan and Vinny enjoyed a bath and then kept up with the sex sessions together watching the money roll in going to the pub enjoying a drink together regularly with Ghianu, Casey, Carol and Colin talking to everybody about how they would love Megan and Vinny's life.

<u>Enjoy story two that is next.</u>

The pub

Chapter One

Tina and Jane pretended to be together

"Hi my name is Tina, I have got brown eyes and blond hair, and I am five foot six with a slim build, I live in a one-bedroom flat on my own and I have decided to go down to the pub with my best friend Jane that lives in the flat above me for my twenty-third birthday, I feel upset that I have not met that special bloke as yet to spend my life with to spoil and look after me."

Jane knocked on Tina's home front door, then walked inside with them enjoying a few drinks together with Tina complimenting Jane about her pink hair with it matching her slim figure before they went to the Head and Toe pub down the road.

They talked while walking to the Head and Toe pub, they then walked inside, as they had arrived, they noticed that it was warm, so Tina decided to open the window to let in some cool air.

Her friend Jane spoke. "That good-looking black-haired fella has just been looking and talking about you, I heard him mention your short red dress when you turned your head to open the window!"

Tina explained. "I can't be bothered; nothing will happen anyway with nothing happening as yet!"

Tina dragged Jane out of the pub, wanting to go to another pub.

Tina and Jane went into town; they entered inside lots of different pubs and pretended to be a couple together cuddling each other.

Some people commented how they looked to be a nice couple, and they mentioned that it was a shame that they fancied each other instead of men.

Tina commented. "It is obvious that they only want a one-night stand with them being drunk, but he has got a nice, toned body, I could quite easily get up very close and under the covers with him, uh la la!"

Jane suggested. "It might be because we are always pretending to be together sexually, maybe this is why we cannot meet a man!"

They went back home after the disco, dancing

together most of the
evening.

The next day they
decided to go horse riding
after cleaning out their
horses that were at a stables
around the corner, as they
were finally sitting on the
horses riding along, they
noticed the same black-
haired chap from the Head
and Toe pub that they had
previously noticed.

Tina just smiled and
then carried on their long
horse ride, hoping to meet a

man while on their horses to make it simple.

They rode the horses back to the stables while discussing that they both needed a gent to stick their fat dicks inside of their clits to feel the amazing sensation of them moving in and out, they then went back home feeling disappointed and let down after their chat.

Tina went for a walk around town noticing a cute white pair of baby mittens, she could not resist not buying them, hoping to meet Mr Right for her and have a baby together, putting them in her bedroom drawer when she got home.

The next day Tina texted Jane most of the day organising to meet at a different pub around the corner called Movers next to the Head, and Toe pub that they went into a few days before.

Jane noticed the same bloke looking at Tina again from a few nights before in the Head and Toe pub, with him trying to get Tina to sit with him and his friends.

Tina would not sit with them and decided to leave and go back to Tina's house.

The bloke followed them out of the Mover's pub and asked Tina and Jane if they would sit with them and have a drink together.

The guy that liked Tina introduced himself as Adam.

Adam introduced his friends Alan and Fred to Tina and Jane.

Tina and Jane introduced themselves, and they sat together on the soft fabric brown bench.

Adam and Tina could not stop talking between each other, with her touching his short black hair and commenting on how nice it felt, with them discussing anything and everything, immediately clicking with a spark

**between them, with them
not really joining in with
Fred, Jane, and Alan.**

Chapter Two

What does bondage feel like

Jane chatted with Alan and Fred, with their discussions getting louder.

Jane liked both Alan and Fred, they liked her as well.

Jane wanted a date with both of them, asking when she could meet up with them.

Alan explained that they were all brothers.

Jane chose to meet up with Fred, explaining that his eyes looked like the blue sea and his lips were fulfilled and cute.

Fred and Jane had a date at a restaurant called Delights, with Tina and Adam sitting at another table.

After they had finished eating, they rang Alan and invited him for a drink with them.

They went off together, meeting up all of the time regularly.

Tina mentioned that her parents had met at the scouts when they were both scout leaders volunteering.

Jane announced that they just needed to help Alan to find a date.

Adam dared Tina to walk in the dark woods at the side of the large lake with him near to his home, she joined him with them finding it a little difficult in the dark not being able to see properly, they stopped at the side of a tree with them starting to kiss and Tina unzipped Adam's trousers letting his disco stick fly out with it rock hard, with them both explaining to each other that it was their first time having sex, and they were looking forward to learning what to do for the first time together.

Tina mentioned. "I wonder what bondage feels like?"

Adam sounded happy. "There is a torch behind you on the tree, drop your pants, and I will whip you on the bottom with it while I finger you!"

Tina announced. "I have dropped my knickers, and I have pulled my dress up!"

Adam asked. "How does bondage feel with my fingers going inside of you as well?"

Tina mentioned. "A
little bit exciting because it
is different!"

Adam gave Tina the
torch.

Tina announced. "I will
spank your bottom with it!"

After a while, she put
the torch back into the tree.

Tina sounded excited.
"I will suck and lick your
dick, Adam, for a long time,
then I will stand up and
open my legs while you

kneel down and lick me out!"

There was a wood bench at the side of them that Tina had noticed.

Adam asked Tina. "Lay down on the bench and I will push my dick inside of your clit to give us lots of babies, I hope!"

Adam thought that Tina was joking, pushing his rock-hard penis inside of Tina's cum hole gently, announcing how lovely, warm, wet, and tight it felt.

Tina suggested. "I am really enjoying your manhood inside of me, it feels all lovely and tingly and amazing as you fill me, I am orgasming everywhere." With her shouting out for more vigorous and fast thrusts.

Adam said that he was glad that his first time enjoying sex was with her, with Tina saying the same back to him.

Adam announced that he was getting close to his

climax pushing his warm wide and long cock in and out fast, with Tina soaking wet with so much cum juice coming out of her fanny making his dick move in nice and deep in and out very smoothly.

They took a breather, doing it by hand for a while, then he shoved his cock between her tits for a while, then Adam rammed his dick back inside of Tina's hole, making excited noises like. "Ohhh, I love your body." And other comments.

Adam asked. "Is it okay to shoot my cum up you still? I feel like I am doing a good job to soak you through with your orgasm juices flowing well?"

Tina mentioned. "Yes, please cum up inside of me, this is amazing, your dick makes me completely feel full filled with it being so wide, I need this every day, and I am completely satisfied with it feeling magical as well!"

Adam sounded excited. "It would be even more magical if I got you pregnant!"

Tina sounded erotic. "I can feel the penetration from the cum releasing from you into me, I love this feeling, it feels magical!"

Adam sounded relieved. "That was amazing, let's get dressed and go home!"

Tina laughed. "I will use some of those leaves to mop myself up!"

Adam sounded a little concerned. "I hope that there are no insects on that leaf that will crawl inside of your pussy!"

Tina screamed. "I can feel something crawling up near to my clit, please get it off me!"

Adam panicked. "I will use the torch to look to see if I can get rid of it for you!"

A lady appeared asking them for the time, she looked at them in disgust and strange asking what they were doing, with her staring at Tina's clit, with it lit up like the limelight on a stage?

They just looked at her speechless.

She explained that she was the caretaker, putting her torch over them, explaining that she looked after the lake and the woods.

Adam made an excuse saying that they had gone the wrong way.

The lady spoke. "That does not explain why you are pant-less!"

Laughing.

Adam suggested. "We went for a bit of naughty play and now Tina has got an insect stuck near to her pussy!"

Tina mentioned. "Adam is helping me to get it out!"

Adam announced. "I think that I have got rid of the insect!"

Adam pulled Tina's knickers up, he put the torch back, he then kissed her.

The lady spoke. "I feel like a gooseberry being left out; I want my man to enjoy sex with me when I get home!"

Pointing them in the exit direction, still laughing to herself.

They walked off with a dirty mark on Adam's trousers from the tree, with the stranger looking at them as they walked off.

Tina sounded a little unhappy. "That was a little bit embarrassing, why did the woodcutter threaten to cut the tree down with his eyes?"

Adam asked. "What is the answer?"

Tina answered. "Because he saw it."

Adam laughed. "Very funny."

Chapter Three

Tina and Adam's bedroom

They walked back to Tina's home after a good sleep in the brief time that they had been together, all that they talked about was wanting to do was live together because they felt like they had been together longer.

Adam moved in with Tina with them feeling incredibly happy together.

Tina started eating strange combinations of food, with her deciding to do a pregnancy test, and she found out that she was pregnant, looking and feeling over the moon, with her looking happy with a smile on her face, wondering how to tell Adam the good news.

Tina remembered that she had bought some baby mittens that she thought were cute weeks before, hoping to get pregnant and feeling excited to use them soon.

Adam felt glad that he had moved in with Tina, finding out that she was pregnant finally, with her putting the positive pregnancy test on to the pair of white tiny wool baby mittens onto the kitchen side that she had bought previously a while back when she was hoping to get pregnant.

Jane and Fred realised how much they liked each other, kissing together on the sofa, playing with one another.

Jane touched Fred tenderly, turning him on.

Fred sounded sexily erotic. "I am loving touching you back Jane and fingering you, I will put my cock inside of you in a minute!"

Jane sounded happy. "Fred thrust in and out of me to make my cum hole wetter, and then you can spurt inside of me!"

Fred announced. "I am spurting inside of you now!"

They sat together watching television having a discussion, deciding to go on holiday together to the seaside with Alan volunteering to drive the friends.

They travelled together in Alan's car with Jane, Adam and Tina sitting in the back.

Jane nodded off to sleep.

Adam covered his and Tina's lap with his black

jacket with him putting his hands down her trousers tickling and fingering her between her legs, he then put his other hand down her top playing with her breasts, while she discretely unzipped his trousers releasing his hard long knob and moved her hands up and down on his dick making him ejaculate all over his jacket.

They arrived with Jane noticing and questioning what the stain was on his jacket, suggesting that it looked like spunk.

Adam announced.
"Yes, it is my cum, you were asleep, so we made the most of the car journey! "

Jane looked a little puzzled. "Okay, it sounds interesting!"

They went up to their room, then unpacked and explored the hotel, going straight into the swimming pool for a swim together.

Alan was talking to a young lady while swimming along about his own age that he fancied the pants off.

The girl introduced herself as Rose.

Rose teased Alan floating her body on top of the water making him beg to kiss her, with her eventually letting him start to kiss her all over, they then swam into the corner of the swimming pool and kissed more with Alan moving the bottom of her costume to one side, he then pushed his long thick tool up Rose's hole.

Everybody was swimming along, staring at them in shock at what they were doing.

After they had finished enjoying sex together, they left the pool with Alan introducing Rose to Tina, Jane, Fred, and Adam, with them sat in the playground drinking cider together, listening to the music from the disco next door enjoying the music while talking.

They decided to go up to Tina and Adam's

bedroom together to enjoy a bit of fun with them all kissing, they then went on sucking the men, with the men fingering them, the men then gave the ladies a foot massage, all in synchronised time with each other.

The ladies sucked the men's cocks, and they then put their cocks inside of their warm holes with them all moaning erotically together about how much they were enjoying each other on the bed.

The men were announcing that they were coming to their crowning point, ejaculating into the ladies.

They laid on the bed chatting, and they decided to go to a football match.

Rose expressed her opinion. "That sounds like fun Alan, let's go!"

They all agreed. Alan drove them there, they had many alcoholic drinks with it being half time, they then went to buy some more drinks while Jane announced that she was pregnant as well, they enjoyed the rowdy football match with the massive buzz that they got from the crowd.

Alan then drove to laser fun near their homes where there were pretend guns that shows a light on each other and it shows up on your backpack that has got lots of different coloured lights on it that you have to wear to show your score, as soon as they entered the big photography room, they all

had a photo together, they
then started to laser each
other, they all found a
corner and kissed getting
told off by the staff for
insensitive behaviour to
others with Jane mentioning
that they were probably
jealous of them with them
agreeing.

Chapter Four

They had a moving-in party with shenanigans.

They travelled back home in the car after their holiday in Alan's extra-large car with Rose also, and they had a general conversation.

Jane shared with everybody that her parents had met at a dance hall, and they were still happy together, and she hoped that she would be like them.

Fred and Jane moved
in together with help from
Adam and Tina.

Rose and Alan got a
flat with them having a
moving-in party inviting
Fred, Jane, Adam, and
Tina.

They enjoyed too much
to drink, like a happy
family enjoying kissing,
touching, licking, and
putting their knobs inside of
them, with the windows
getting steamed up, with
them getting so hot and

raunchy, with their cocks moving in and out so fast.

Rose suddenly announced to everybody that she was pregnant as well.

They sat outside and enjoyed barbecues with plenty of food and drink at Rose and Alan's new home.

Alan commented. "My parents met in a queue on Boxing Day while entering a shop for the sales, and they are still together as well."

They explored the two-bedroom home with it beautifully kitted out with everything that you could imagine.

They all set up a gym between them with hot tubs and a swimming pool employing staff, and they were never out of the hot tubs together, their new business made them well off with plenty of money.

The ladies felt like someone, or something, was fluttering about in their stomachs like butterflies, with a fluttering feeling inside, it was strange, but a nice, strange sensation turning into a kick in the stomach as the babies got larger.

In the sauna, they decided to massage each other with the unborn babies starting to kick inside a little more.

Tina went into labour, pushing baby Nichola out.

Not long after, Jane went into labour with baby Dan being born.

Weeks later, Rose gave
birth to baby David.

The babies grew up
and went to school with
them enjoying each others
company and playing
together.

Their kids enjoyed
birthday parties and went
to school together.

They made the best
individual unique parents,
not realising how hard but
rewarding it would be to be
a parent.

Nichola asked why
people kissed.

They explained that
they love each other.

Nicola went around
kissing people in nursery
school, including the
teacher, not really
understanding what her
mum, Tina, had meant.

The nursery teacher
told Tina that she had
mentioned to Nichola that
she could not go around

kissing everybody, she
understood.

While Nichola was at
nursery school, in their
home, Adam started to
remove Tina's pants, licking
her pussy out, then fingered
her with him feeling eager
for his knob inside of her.

There was a knock at
the door.

Tina answered with
Rose, Alan, Jane, and Fred
at the door walking inside.

They all stripped off together, touching each other as partners, they then licked each other with them enjoying bondage, with a flower as a whip each, whipping each other with them getting covered in petals.

They then fingered and tugged each other off at the same time, they then slipped their dicks in their holes thrusting in and out, with them all suggesting that it would be nice to have more kids running about.

They started to have
sex parties charging people
for entering inside of their
homes, with a different
home for people attending a
party each time, with the
words on the advert saying.
'This is a learn how to enjoy
each others' bodies party!'

Babysitters looked
after the children with
everybody walking out with
a smile on their faces, with
them discussing how many
people they had slept with
and explained that they
would be attending again
the next time that another

party was running with them saying how much fun they had and how tired they felt, with them making sure that they had their moneys worth, having their dicks sucked more than ever before, and they had enjoyed their dicks inside many of the opposite sex.

Enjoy story three next.

Foam parties.

Chapter One

Greg and James' faces lit up as Emma and Lucy walked in

" Hi, my name is Greg, I am tall and slim with blond hair!"

"Hi, my name is James, I am not as tall as Greg, I love my short black hair and super white teeth!"

Greg mentioned. "We always sit in the sun together to top up our tan in between going on the sun beds, James is my good friend!"

James announced. "We are both twenty years old, and we go into town regularly to different places with us longing to meet a sweet lady to spend the rest of our lives with!"

Greg sounded shy. "Every time that we go into town, we find it difficult to speak with a lady because we are both far too shy!"

James shared. "We both work at a local law firm full time, and we have got dirty pictures and dirty magazines of women in our private draws in our desks!"

Greg mentioned. "We regularly lock our public work front door for a while, while we toss ourselves off over the women with our dicks facing over the magazines and discuss how good-looking that they look, and we always hope that one day we could have a real naked woman with the amount of spunk on our magazines!"

James laughed. "The only problem is that it is getting harder to open them because the pages are getting stuck together!"

Greg smiled. "We help each other out with jobs and advice as needed, our clients are from many different backgrounds!"

James mentioned. "We go down to the local gym every dinnertime for lunch

and a small workout, and
on an evening occasionally!"

Greg announced.
"When we are at the gym, I
can't help but look at a girl
called Lucy that visits the
gym as much as us, she is
slim, and tall, and her big
tits are so wow, and her
blond long hair is so cute,
and there are a few freckles
on her face that are
beautiful, and she is about
my own age, she is there
most times that we go, every
time that we go to the gym,
I just want to remove her
pants if she had any on and

undress her with my eyes imagining me sticking my cock inside of her, but I am too shy to talk with her, I only know her name because I have heard someone say her name before!"

James mentioned. "I like a girl called Emma that also visits the gym with her being short, slim, and she has got short brown hair, I was too shy to speak to her also, but I found out her name in the same way!"

Greg stared. "We are in the gym now, I have just noticed Emma and Lucy speaking to each other only steps away from us, I have just realised that they are friends!"

Back in Greg and James's office.

James put the phone down. "A new lady client has just rang asking if we could chat in person now with them about them needing help as they were moving house!"

Greg announced. "Our new clients are about to walk in; I can hear their footsteps!"

Emma and Lucy walked into the office with Greg and James's faces lighting up like a light bulb to see them.

They asked for advice and help for them moving house.

Greg and James explained what they needed to do, attempting to keep the conversation official with Lucy and Emma understanding what they needed to do.

They gave details about where they were moving to, and where they were moving from.

As Emma and Lucy were about to leave, they started to talk about how they had seen Greg and James in the gym, explaining that they always wanted to chat with them.

James asked if Emma and Lucy were officially together.

Emma explained. "It is the only way that we can afford to buy a house together, but we are not a couple!"

They started talking to each other.

Emma and Lucy commented that they both liked them, and they were always talking about them in the gym, thinking that

James and Greg were together.

James announced. "We have always liked and wished that we were with you, Emma and Lucy."

Greg sounded a little nervous. "All that we could do was watch you in the gym from a distance!"

James sounded a little nervous. "We were longing to speak with you for a while, but we couldn't pluck up the courage to!"

Greg sounded over-happy. "It is like all of our dreams have come true all at once!"

They organised a night out together at Lucy and Emma's home having plenty to drink, Greg sat with Lucy, mainly talking to her.

Emma spoke mainly with James, with them getting very tipsy.

Chapter Two

Emma and Lucy teased them

Emma and Lucy got a little carried away, starting to kiss the men, with them getting excited, asking if that was what they really wanted.

They both nodded up and down, saying. "Definitely yes please!"

Emma announced. "I have fancied the pants off you, James, for ages!"

Lucy then commented. "I have fancied you, Greg, for a long time, you are so good-looking, I feel like ripping your clothes off every time that I see you!"

Emma replied. "I have got a joke; how do you make a pool table laugh?"

Lucy asked. "What is the answer?"

Emma answered. "Tickle its balls!"

Greg replied. "Very funny."

Emma and Lucy were in control and started to remove their own clothes and then started to strip the mens clothes off, and then sucked the mens hot rods, struggling to fit them in their mouths a little with them being so fat and long.

The men sucked their tits, showing that they had never had sex before because they were so eager to stick their warm lollies inside of their warm very moist clits.

Emma and Lucy teased them, putting their rock-hard cocks near their holes with it being their first time as well.

Emma smiled. "I will count down when I will sit on you, James, and put your hard as a rock cum rod inside of me!"

She counted down three, two, and one, she then slowly sat on his penis, with Lucy doing the same to Greg.

They were rolling
about all over the floor on
top of each other, having a
fun time.

Emma and Lucy teased
Greg and James by putting
their dicks in between their
tits, moving up and down
with their cocks, still in
between their warm breasts.

Greg and James then
put their pricks back inside
of them getting hot and
sweaty with them
announcing that they were
both about to spurt their
love juice up inside of their

warm holes, with them all saying hurray as their cum juices flowed into them, with them enjoying feeling the lovely penetration from it shooting into them, they shared how much they had enjoyed it.

Greg noticed that there was a large old warehouse for sale over the road where they were moving house to suggesting to turn it into a foam party disco, and one day a week as an adult-only sex session so that other people could meet their future loved ones.

Lucy, James, and Emma agreed, deciding to have a double wedding as soon as they had moved house.

Greg and James helped Lucy and Emma to move house with them moving in with them, they had their own parties, with them having regular sex at the same time as each other in the same room, with them all putting their money together purchasing the building and turned it into a foam party.

They had many parties for years, with many people meeting the right person that they wanted to spend the rest of their lives with thanking them for helping their romance happen.

They hoped that Lucy and Emma would be pregnant soon and have a family enjoying life together.

Greg and Fred gave up their jobs and employed staff to help them run the foam parties.

The parties run all day and night with them being exceedingly popular, with people attending from far away and close to home.

They enjoyed life together and were happy that they had finally met someone that they loved with people knocking at their door often asking them to join in with the foam sex parties with bondage sessions, and they put blindfolds on peoples eyes with special long whips available to whip peoples naked bottoms and they wore fluffy handcuffs with people begging for sex.

They were both pregnant at the same time announcing their news to Greg and James at their own private party, with them feeling over the moon with their happy news with them still enjoying sex together with milk coming from their boobs into Greg, and James's mouths when they had sucked their breasts, announcing that the breast milk tasted strange, but it did not put them off right up to the day that they had given birth.

They attended plenty of sex parties having sex in the middle of everybody dancing around them, and some people had sex around them with people enjoying watching them lick each other all over and caress each other getting a massive turned-on sex buzz, with a babysitter-looking after the children regularly while they went to join in with the sex parties.

They had their double wedding in their foam party building with everyone invited, with every photo of them covered in foam with a kid-friendly area that they had built for the children to play in, with the babysitter looking after many children while the parent customers enjoyed themselves.

Enjoy story four next.

Fun or not.

Chapter One

Is it a free day trip for a reason?

Shirley and Frank were more than friends regularly having sex sessions, with them deciding to go on holiday together as friends, as they had all of the time in the world since they had won the lotto to visit many places in the world because they had shared a lotto ticket and won big on the lotto.

Their families were jealous and happy for them at the same time.

They made a will, leaving their money to certain family members informing them.

Shirley commented to Frank that she had left her money to her brother, Graham.

Graham was friends with Frank's sister, Sue whom Frank had willed his money to.

Sue did not have much money and regularly commented that she would love to have as much as him.

Shirley and Frank noticed that Sue and Graham were talking a lot together more than usual recently with Shirley and Frank thinking that they were a couple.

Graham recommended Hotel Company to Shirley and Frank.

Shirley booked the holiday for them to go to the Hotel Company that Graham had recommended.

They got to their hotel called Hotel Company, they went to their room ripping each others clothes off, then Shirley sucked his cock enjoying every second feeling how hard his cock was, he touched her tits passionately, and Frank then licked Shirley's pussy out, while he put his fingers up her anus, they then massaged each other gently making each other jump all over the bed with each others fingers tickling them, Frank then put his dick into Shirley's clit with her enjoying every thrust making the bed bang onto the wall really hard, and it was making a large squeaking noise every time that Frank thrust inside of her.

There was a knock on the door.

Frank put on the dressing gown on that Hotel Company had provided answering the door.

The people from next door were standing at the door complaining about the squeaking and banging noise from them enjoying sex, explaining that they were asleep.

Frank announced. "We will not be much longer; do you know what the recipe is for honeymoon salad?"

The people at the door replied. "No, we don't know."

Frank answered. "Lettuce alone without dressing!"

He then shut the door with him dropping his dressing gown to the floor.

Shirley laughed. "That was funny."

Frank then got back on top of Shirley, making the bed squeak again, with it sounding like the wall was going to cave in, they were coming to their crowning point with Frank ejaculating inside of Shirley.

They left their cases inside of the door saying that they would unpack later, they then went downstairs to enjoy themselves in the sun by the pool.

Shirley overheard a guest talking to a member of staff saying that it will be worth getting rid of her to get all of her money and everything that she owns to have her lush and lavish life.

The guests at the side of Shirley and Frank that

had just been talking with Shirley listening to their conversation, they then got up and left, noticing that Shirley was listening to their conversation and looked at her as they walked off.

Holidaymakers in the hotel with Shirley and Frank discussed among each other about the conversation that Shirley had heard how bad it sounded, with it sounding like the hotel was offering to kill people off for money, with them saying that the only solution was for them to keep their eyes open for any criminal behaviour occurring, debating if they should have phoned the police in case they were the victims of a crime that hadn't happened as yet, with them deciding to gather more evidence first.

The staff behind the reception desk offered Shirley and Frank a free trip out for the day by the tour excursion lady behind a till that only a selected few that they had chosen could go on the free trip, with a limited amount of coach seats available explaining that they would be painting some miniature houses for a charity, and they would get a mention in the newspaper for their help.

Shirley noticed the written sign on the front of the coach saying house painting day trip.

A coach load of sixty holidaymakers, including Shirley and Frank got onto the coach noticing that they had arrived at the private airport.

They entered onto a plane, then onto a train, and then a bus to get to their destination.

It was supposed to be an enjoyable day trip out painting.

They were all moaning that they were hungry.

As they arrived at the building, they noticed a sign saying. 'Fun.'

As their coach arrived, they noticed people looking clean and happy, enjoying a civilised meal through the window on their way in.

They sat in a different separate room from the people that they had noticed on the way inside through the window.

They enjoyed a hot meal served to them.

Shirley mentioned. "I hope that it is worth it, I have got a gut feeling that something isn't as it should be because alarm bells are ringing in my head with different dark scary clues appearing, I hope that I am wrong!"

Frank laughed. "At least there are no elevators, because sex is wrong on so many levels."

Shirley laughed. "Very funny."

They were asked to put their belongings into lockers, with them putting their personal things inside of the lockers using their thumb or fingerprint to lock them.

Shirley questioned the man that was asking them to put their items inside of the lockers. "Why do we need to lock our items up to paint?"

The man started sweating, replying. "I have never been asked this before; it is just so that you don't get paint on your things or lose them or trip over them!"

Shirley spoke. "I will keep my things, thank you!"

The man replied. "No, put your items in the locker, or you can't go in!"

Shirley reluctantly put her items in the locker.

The man opened the door, they then walked into a strange room with no windows, with them looking around noticing a large circular obstacle course with large boxes to climb over and there were planks of wood for people to walk on, with books at the side of the room and some were stuck inside of gaps in the high ceiling with the room large enough for them to spread out and move around freely.

Frank agreed. "I think that you may be correct Shirley, there are no houses to paint in here, it is a dodgy, unexplainable situation!"

Shirley sounded upset. "It looks like we are all doomed, there is no way out, I feel frightened!"

They looked strange around the room; every obstacle had a large bucket

of green slime at the end of
it.

A man introduced
himself as Jack who arrived
with them in the room from
a door, he explained that
was the activity instead as
the other activity painting
houses had been cancelled
and it was a fun obstacle
course for them, he then left
the room locking them
inside.

Frank spoke. "The
man who invented the
automatic door deserves a
no-bell prize!"

Shirley laughed. "Very
funny."

They walked on a round circular obstacle course avoiding the slime, they could not see the point of this obstacle course, some people thought that it was fun.

The people that asked to leave got told over the tannoy that there would be one winner at the end with no more explanation.

They got fed up with walking around and nearly falling, getting slime on them from other people with them trying to brush it off unsuccessfully.

Suddenly most of the ceiling started to transport down for them to enter up some steep steps, then into a large open red slide from the high roof, with a large shallow bucket of green slime at the bottom, with some people finding the room a little bit more interesting looking at it.

Shirley shared her thoughts. "There is definitely something fishy going on here with Jack locking the door and leaving us to it, I want you to stay close to me Frank, please!"

Frank sounded loving. "I will stay close to you, I

am concerned as well for our and everyone else's safety that came with us on the coach, with what you heard earlier by the pool with the hotel trying to kill people off and what sits at the bottom of the sea and twitches?"

Shirley asked. "What is the answer?"

Frank answered. "A nervous wreck."

Shirley smiled. "Yes, that is us at the moment."

Chapter Two

They enjoyed each other thinking that it was their last moments alive

Ten people went down the open red slide with green bags coming from above them, with them ending up around their heads and a string around their necks pulling tight, it was like the bags had been put on by a person but had somehow automatically appeared.

Everybody else was crying because the victims were suffocating, and they could not help because they

were too slimy with their
hands sliding off the bag
and the rope.

People shouted to Jack
crying. "If this is fun, come
and get suffocated
yourself!"

Frank looked up.
"Looking up, I have noticed
the nearly invisible string
that blended in with the
room attached to the slime
bags, with a separate string
to pull the rope around
their necks, that was so
sneakily dangerous!"

They all sat down and
joined Shirley and Frank,
discussing how to get out.

Shirley explained that she realised that there was something going on when Jack had locked them inside and the man had started sweating, with clues adding together.

They all said the same, still tearful.

Suddenly a heavy iron block came down from the ceiling fast onto a box that ten of them were sitting on opposite Shirley and Frank crushing them to death, it then went back up to the ceiling with blood dripping down from the iron block like it was rain.

The victims that were
left were terribly upset,
crying even harder for their
lives, leaving only forty of
them left.

They sat on the floor
full of blood and green
slime, discussing what they
should do next, with some
people banging on the door
to let them go.

Some people wrote a
message on the wall using
the green slime writing. 'We
hope that you die also,
Jack.'

They did not know
what to do slipping about

underfoot as they walked around in a raging panic for their lives.

Five people that were banging on the door and the five that were leaning on the door suddenly got an electric shock with it nearly killing them making them go into a fit with their bodies shaking erratically, then it immediately killed them with them falling to the floor lifeless.

The others dare not touch them because they were scared of getting a shock as well, with them feeling distraught and full of anger.

Shirley commented while crying. "There are only thirty of us left, this is a terrible situation!"

Twenty people started to bang on the walls attempting to get attention from the people outside, as they banged on the wall they fell inside of the wall like it was made out of what it looked like a mixture of marshmallows and butter-sucking them inside, with their top half inside of the wall and their legs were left limp in the same place as they had died leaving ten of them left.

All they could say was who is next and said their goodbyes.

They decided between them to have a sex session, thinking that it was their last moments to live, so they said why not enjoy the last moments remarkably close together?

They stripped their clothes off touching each other up and down, the slime acted as a kind of smooth strange oil making it feel smooth massaging each other, with the men sticking their fingers in their vaginas, the men licked the ladies' clits

pulling a funny face with
the strange taste of slime in
their mouths, then the men
slipped their cocks inside of
the women putting it in
faster and faster struggling
to keep on top and not slide
off ejaculating their cum
into the ladies.

They put their clothes
back on with a struggle,
watching a torrent wave of
slime enter under the
entrance door fast.

They ran away as fast
as they could to the large
red slide with six of them
falling and getting covered
in slime from head to foot,

making them drown in the
slime.

There were only four of
them left, including Shirley
and Frank.

Chapter Three

Do the last four survive?

They talked among themselves, saying whoever survives needs to stop this situation from happening to other people.

Shirley explained. "I think that the people that we noticed eating and looking like they were enjoying themselves on the way into the building, they must be survivors from this obstacle course in this building made into prisoners, or they are the evil people in charge!"

They all agreed, with Shirley crying and feeling scared.

Suddenly on the red slide where they were sat, it opened up under them with three of them falling into the hole of the slide with screaming noises lasting a while, Shirley just got away in time hearing a loud thud and then a constant scream from the hole that they had fallen into as if one of them had survived, Shirley was hoping that Frank had survived.

Shirley was the only one left alive feeling devastated, distraught, and very uncontrollably upset at everything that had happened hearing the key in the door open with Jack walking in and congratulating Shirley for being the winner.

Shirley was so annoyed hitting Jack for killing her friends and asked to go to get her items from her locker.

Jack had no care laughing at her saying that she would not need them again because she would stay there until she was no use to them anymore then they would kill her, Jack threw her into a shower asking her to get clean and then told her to put on the clothes provided not giving her a towel to dry herself with.

As Shirley had got clean, she was asking why this had happened to her while she was walking along.

Jack replied saying that she was lucky to be alive, and he should not be saying too much to her, he then threw her into a room with two other people inside.

They were distraught the same as her explaining

the similar situations that they had been in, arriving from the Hotel Company, introducing themselves as Polly and Grace, with Shirley introducing herself as well.

They knew that it was possibly something to do with them having plenty of money for their family, friends, or strangers to steal.

Polly also explained that the coach load of people that was killed with her had all been advised to stay at the Hotel Company by family members, or friends.

Grace announced that they only got invited to paint houses because they said that they were special, and they had been chosen out of a lot of hotel guests at the same hotel called Hotel Company with them getting upset.

Shirley explained about the conversation that she heard sitting at the side of the pool with the hotel staff member helping them to get rid of someone for their money.

They knew that it was something to do with the hotel and maybe Graham and Sue wanting their money.

They heard the key in the door with men appearing around the door asking for them to clean the obstacle course room with the men explaining that the bodies were removed.

They were locked inside of the obstacle course room; it took them a long time to clean up with other victims joining them discussing similar situations what had happened to them.

They watched people destroying the wall that Shirley's friends had been inside of, with them putting fresh soft stuff on it for the next victims.

They were not allowed to leave until they had finished realising and discussing that they were only alive to do the cleaning up instead of the people that were in charge doing this to them, putting them into a devastating situation.

Shirley was upset again with it bringing back memories with the others getting upset with her at what had happened.

They discussed ganging up on the guards and

stealing their keys to leave the building and find out what was going on for themselves.

Grace mentioned. "I will use this hard book that I have just found as a weapon!"

As they had finished cleaning, a few male guards unlocked the door and asked them to go back to their rooms.

Grace hit a guard with her book around the head with Polly, Shirley, and the rest of them joining in knocking them to the floor, they then stole their keys

**and locked the guards
inside of the obstacle course.**

Chapter Four

Do they get their own back?

Polly spoke. "You're knocked out, locked up and booked, you can have a taste of your own medicine!"

They went to Shirley's locker hoping that everything was still there, getting her handbag with her purse and other things inside noticing a tool stuck inside of a tiny hole in a locker to open it up saying. 'This opens locked lockers.' With it being left inside of the locker door.

Grace announced. "I have just used the tool to see if it opened other lockers and thankfully, it does work."

Polly sounded distraught. "So that is how they remove peoples' items to give the items to their family members left behind, causing this to happen!"

They unlocked the locker doors and walked outside with a sigh of relief to be alive and free noticing that the coach outside that had brought them to the supposedly fun place had the keys in the ignition with them getting on it, Shirley then drove it to the train station.

Shirley used her cash card with it getting rejected, with them realising that the people from the fun place had worked out that it was hers and they had cancelled her card so that she had no help or resources.

They sat on the floor and begged for extra money from people walking past with them getting just enough to get on to the plane.

As they boarded the plane, they noticed staff

from the fun building on the
runway as they took off.

As the plane arrived,
they hitched a ride with
many kind strangers back
to the Hotel Company.

As they walked inside
of the hotel, the hotel staff
looked at them like they
were shocked that they were
not dead with their mouths
open, and their eyes were
open wide, speaking with a
low tone of voice asking
each other how they were
alive.

Shirley, Polly, Grace,
and other victims got hold
of a staff member from the

hotel demanding to be told
what had happened,
speaking loudly asking how
all of their friends could die
because of what they were
doing.

The hotel staff said that
they were sorry with a tear
rolling down their faces and
they were getting upset as
well.

There was a coach load
of holidaymakers just
getting on to a coach outside
of the hotel with it saying on
the front of it. 'Charity
painting houses day out.'

On a board on the
window, the same as it had
said for them.

Shirley stepped onto
the coach and ordered the
holidaymakers to leave the
coach immediately.

The holiday victims
were all complaining
because they explained that
they were looking forward
to painting houses for a
charity, and they were
having their pictures taken
to be placed in the
newspaper.

Shirley explained that
the same had happened to
them, and they were in

grave danger if they did not leave the coach, and their relatives were trying to kill them for their money, and they would die if they stayed on the coach.

Polly asked people to put their hands up if they have got lots of money or had recently changed their wills.

Every holidaymaker put their hands up and then finally left the coach with them ganging up on the hotel staff making them enter the coach, and have the same treatment from hell that Shirley, Polly,

Grace, and others had gone through.

Shirley noticed her brother Graham and Frank's sister Sue that they had left their money to, with them about to walk out of the reception door with her, and Frank's suitcases thanking the staff for their help looking a little tearful and talking about what they had done.

Shirley looked dirty, tired and very upset, shouting for Graham and Sue not to leave, with Sue and Graham looking around like they had seen a ghost saying that they were

surprised that she was alive
and explained that they
were so sorry for what they
had done to them, saying
that they needed their
money to get out of debt,
and stealing their money
when they had gone it was
the easiest way to make
them rich.

Shirley spoke loudly.
"Get on the coach now, both
of you and all of the staff, or
I will tell the world what
you are doing!"

A holidaymaker from
the hotel asked them if they
had a lovely day out and
asked why she looked and
sounded angry; it was a

hotel guest that Shirley had spoken to previously.

Shirley explained what had happened, and that is why she looked a little worse for wear saying that she would be the next victim, the woman walked off from Shirley looking upset with Shirley grabbing a large ball of string from behind the desk tying the remainder of the staff, Sue, and Graham up on the coach.

The guest that Shirley had just spoken to had collected her things and then left the hotel feeling

upset at what Shirley had
told her.

Polly, Grace and three
people that could have been
future victims volunteered
boarding the coach, helping
Shirley make the remainder
of the people get onto the
coach reluctantly, with
Shirley getting on last, the
coach driver then set off.

Graham and Sue
explained again crying
explaining that they did not
have enough money, so they
searched the internet typing
in how to dispose of a
person, with the fun
building offering everything
that they wanted at a small

cost and explained that they deeply regretted what they had done afterwards.

Shirley explained in a very traumatic upset tone of voice in detail what she had been through and what had happened to Frank and the other victims to Sue, and Graham.

Graham and Sue pleaded with Shirley not to kill them.

Grace collected all of the phones from everyone putting them into a carrier bag, with her using a phone to call the police that she had taken from a staff

member on the coach
asking the police to meet
her at the fun building,
explaining the whole
situation with the police
eager to arrest the hotel
staff.

Grace tied the rest of
the hotel staff up with them
finally arriving at the fun
building after their
nightmare of a journey,
with the hotel staff getting
pushed inside of the
obstacle course room, with
the staff from the fun
building pushing Shirley,
Grace, the other victims and
Polly inside also saying that
they would all die to cover

up what they had been doing.

Grace whispered to Shirley, and Polly saying that they would be okay because the police should be on their way.

A few of the hotel staff were having a panic attack not being able to get their breath, with one of the hotel staff that was apologising to the victims the most introducing himself as Liam explaining that he was in charge of sending who needed disposing of from the paying customers to send them there.

Suddenly a box that they were supposed to jump onto for fun lifted up fast behind Liam, the box then landed on his head, killing him instantly.

Everybody looked distraught, wondering who would be next, but Shirley, Grace and Polly felt a little happier that Liam had got what was coming to him after what he had been doing.

Police unlocked the door and arrested them all, including Graham and Sue working out that Frank, Polly, Shirley, Grace, and the other victims were definitely the victims and witnesses.

The police found all of the bodies in a skip in the back of the building; the police took the surviving victims to it to say their goodbyes.

They noticed some movement in the skip, hearing a faint cry for help.

The police looked inside of the skip noticing that Frank was trying to crawl out of the skip among all of the dead bodies explaining that he was hurt and traumatised, but he had noticed as he first fell that he must have landed on a box full of soft rubbish that he had noticed below him as he fell unconscious, that must have given him a soft landing, explaining that the blood on him must have made him look like he was dead, with him thinking and explaining that he must have definitely been unconscious as the last thing that he remembered was been sat on the slide then falling, explaining that he thought that the staff must have thrown him into the skip.

Frank got taken into hospital for treatment.

The gang of people that ended so many lives for money got locked up for life with the police making sure that they tracked all of the family members down that had caused this to happen, locking them up as well.

The fun building got knocked down, and it was made into a memorial hotel for people that had lost their lives and Frank and Shirley bought the hotel making everyone welcome, with Shirley finding out that she was pregnant telling Frank, they talked about everything that they had gone through to people making it a talking point, telling people to watch out if it is a free trip that it might be too good to be true still having nightmares.

They heard people mentioning that the hotel staff and the fun building staff were being beaten up every day in prison because families, friends, and strangers that might have known them and the people that did not know them attacked them because of what they had done.

But over the years that went by, they enjoyed their child called Jenna and made sure that she was safe, and they enjoyed more making love sessions going alone, not contacting family members again and felt happy to be alive.

The End.

Other books by the author Anita Kirk

About the author

Anita Kirk is from Yorkshire in the United Kingdom, she works full time and writes many book genres in her spare time with unlimited talent to write anything, she loves swimming, line dancing, holidays, music, films, writing, reading, and spending time with friends and family.

All of Anita Kirk's books have got <u>funny moments</u> that may make you feel like laughing your socks off.

**These books have been written
so far with many more
that will be available soon.**

PLEASE·TYPE·ANITA·KIRK·INTO·AMAZON

·FOR·ALL·AVAILABLE·PUBLISHED·BOOKS

·OF·MANY·DIFFERENT·GENRES.·

Remember that you can follow and contact Anita Kirk with any questions or comments on Tick Tock, Facebook, Twitter, LinkedIn or you can email any comments to anitajane1@outlook.com Please contact Anita if you would like a shop opening or anything else and she will get back to you as soon as possible with an answer.
If you have enjoyed reading Anita Kirk's books a good review would be

appreciated and if you could share Anita's books on your social media, and with your family and friends she would really appreciate your help. Thank you for your support in reading this book.
All of Anita Kirk's books are available on Amazon and some other online shops.

A good review would mean a lot if you have enjoyed this book.
Thank you in advance for your good positive review it is very much appreciated.

<u>Erotically Spooky</u> is the <u>same</u> as <u>Spooky Scary</u> but it has got a little bit of raunch, and vampires attempt to take over the world with funny moments to make you laugh out loud.

<u>Thank you.</u>

Anita Kirk, author
@AnitaKi73550337

Twitter –

Author Anita Kirk

LinkedIn-

Instagram-

@anitakirkauthor ▣

You can also follow Anita Kirk on tick tock.

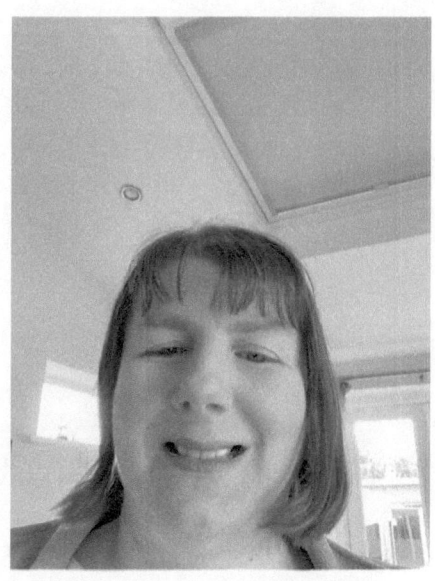